BED 26

BED 26

A Memoir of an African Man's
Asylum in The United States

EDAFE OKPORO

To order additional copies of this book, contact:
Xlibris
1-888-795-4274
www.Xlibris.com
Orders@Xlibris.com
773694

This book is inspired by a true life story.

CONTENTS

Acknowledgment

Thanks to Kevin Rodriguez, who stood by me through the writing process, for providing me with a listening ear, for fighting with me, and for giving me positive reactions and constructive criticism. Thanks to Frances Connell, who accepted to read and edit my first draft. Thanks to my mentor, Tom O'Toole, for reminding me always of the *whys*. Thank you, sir. James V. Ryan, you are my pillar and support, my Pee. I would never forget your support, Kent "Batman" Klindera. Thank you, Emily Kullman, Christina Rodriquez Hart, and Lilian and Summer Mckee—the women of virtue.

There are too many to mention. Thanks to my contributors who want to remain anonymous. Thank you, CJ, Asylees, First Friends of New Jersey and New York, Immigration Equality, and to my lawyers from Debevoise and Plimpton.

Thank you to my mothers—Alice Akanusi, Igho Akanusi, and Grace Erhimona. Your support saw me through difficult times.

Give sorrow words.
—William Shakespeare

A Lamentation for the Dead

There are many women who have provided me support in my life—my mother and my Aunty Grace. These women were resilient, my definition of strong African women, but I would not end my story without letting you know the role of my grandmother—Mrs. Alice Akanusi. I wrote this letter to her.

> Dear granny, although you are dead your memories forever live in my heart. When I walk through this lonely earth I remember you always and I wish you were still alive. Your prayers are yea and amen, and indeed your legacy of love is unconditional. Your prayers for me to succeed were the only push I had when others thought I was not going to make it out of college.
>
> I remembered you granny, I remembered how you gathered up your savings, from the little box under your bed and gave to me, and said, "Buy some food and study hard." At other times you loosened your cloth (wrapper) from your waist and tied it around me, pampering me like a baby from your womb.
>
> Night and day your prayers were guarding me, you wake up in the middle of the night, walk silently into my room, sit and watch me sleep like a baby. I woke up to the reality of blood stains on my wall, asking my mum how come my wall is blood filled and she replied you where there last night killing mosquitoes and preventing my tender skin from harm. Times when I fall sick of malaria you prepared some herbs and ties around my head. What on earth is more precious than the unconditional love you had for me?
>
> You were the only woman that said to me "I love you Nong." I know you were strong enough to work, you washed my clothes, you never wanted my stomach to feel empty. You always shared your meals with me, making sure I had meat and fish, because I needed protein to grow

my fragile, youthful bones. You were willing to back me with your wrapper and walk me to school so my feet would not touch the floor.

When it is time to go to school, I would run to your door to say, "Mama am going to school." One morning I ran to your room but the feeling was unusual, and I stopped at the door and placed my ear on the door just to listen to your voice. I peeped through your key hole and saw you on your knees with my picture in your hands. I didn't know what you were doing but I knew you too well not to disturb your prayers. I love you, I miss you and hold on to the memories of your sweet smiling face.

Mama, the world is different from when you were in it, I am no longer a little boy. I have grown to acknowledge your support and prayers. I only wish you were alive to see that your prayer is now a reality, your prayer for me to break the cause of having a college degree, as I am now a college graduate. Even so, some of the money you contributed to me for my daily care in school was taken by blackmailers who victimized me because of my sexuality.

I am now in a distant country, thousands of miles from your grave, but the day I heard of your death I almost ran into the high way. I had a strange feeling that day before I got the news, and I was wearing a black shirt and pants. I called your daughter, my mother, to ask her about you, but she refused to tell me of your death because she knows the bond we share. It was few weeks to my final college exams, and when I finally got to know about it my world never remained the same. I wish you could have held on and seen me running home to present my Bachelor's degree.

The day you were finally laid to rest, I stood by your coffin. I looked for tears but I could not weep. Instead, I ended up smiling, and I know you were up there smiling too. You lived a beautiful life, you are a virtuous woman, a true African mother, who raised seven children and ten grandchildren. Of which I am proudly one.

Mama!!! Your values will live forever.

Now I feel better than I did in my past. The only thing I could have done differently was to be able to confide in you about my struggles. I know despite all the world put you through, you still held on to your faith. When your husband, my late grandfather, married other women after you, ending up chasing you away in your old age, I still heard you pray for him every morning. When I heard how you died, I left you with praises; you died peacefully in the arms of your daughter, my mother.

You are one of a kind, Death is cruel, for there are people you wish live forever and one of them is you.

In loving memory of my grandmother, Mrs. Alice Akanusi.

CHAPTER ONE

The Day I Met My Doom

Silence is important but our stories cannot be kept silent because that would prevent people from knowing the struggle we have gone through.
—Nong Richie

I am the only one who can tell the story of my life and say what it means.
—Dorothy Allison

"Okay, faggot, get ready to die." These were the words my kidnappers used to place me in a still state. I was kidnapped by four men who had no mercy; these men were ready to kill.

In July 2014, I traveled to eastern Nigeria to pick up my call letter to know the state I was posted to for my National Youth Service Corps (NYSC). I had to go to the college where I graduated. I arrived at Enugu a day before the posting letters were distributed, and I spent the night with my colleagues and ex-classmates, smiling and sharing memories of the good old days of college, when I had gone around campaigning for their votes and consequently showed resilience in winning the student union elections as the first nonindigenous student union president of my department.

I woke up the next morning, eager to end my visit in Enugu, pick up the letter, and run home to prepare for National Youth Service Corps (NYSC). When I arrived at school, I could hear the birds singing. It was that early. My friends arrived, and we went through the long lines of the bursary unit to certify we didn't owe the institution a penny. I could not leave Agbani, Enugu, that day till about 5:00 p.m. because of the strenuous administrative procedures and the long queues to go through. I decided to break my journey in two—spend the night at the park in Asaba and continue my journey the following day. A few hours from home, Asaba is located in Delta State, Nigeria. At the same time, I knew my family awaited the homecoming of their first college graduate.

I waited at this horrible park. A bright light bulb overhead was attracting insects, and my feet in the dark had been fed on by mosquitoes. I received a text from the guy whom I had told earlier I would be passing through Asaba. I had told him I might spend the night in Asaba because I was running late, and he asked me in a text message if I had gotten home. *Oh, that's generous of him*, I thought. I replied, "No, am sleeping in the park." And he graciously offered for me to come spend the night in his place. Who would sleep in that park and suffer all night when you have the option of lying in a sofa inside?

I had earlier been warned by friends not to meet anyone in the Asaba area, but I did not listen to what my friends had gossiped about because of my condition that night. The address he sent me was in Ibuzor, Delta State, a town very close to Asaba but not actually in Asaba. I got off the bus, which took about fifteen minutes from Asaba to Ibuzor, and called him. He sent an *okada* to pick me up. The guy on the motorcycle drove me into the dark—as usual, a small community with no electricity and with few lampstands—but my mind was not troubled because that was a usual setting in most Nigerian villages.

Then the next sound I heard was a slap on my face.

"Hey, get down from the okada, bloody faggot."

The guy who slapped me was their leader, joined by three other men, who told me that this was my last day on planet Earth. This guy was prepared, and the beating started with sticks that were plucked from branches close by. Soon they were throwing anything they could find on the ground on me, especially stones. Their leader's voice was not that bold, but it still carried a lot of power. He said to me in pidgin English, "If you make any noise, we go kill you and leave your body for this bush." I was not afraid because I thought, *I have met my doom*. This would be the last day my parents would see me, my family who was happy that the last child had broken the curse and was going to NYSC. All hope of my family having a child with a college degree had been lost because of my identity. These men beat me up and pushed me onto the road. They were waiting for a truck to run over me. Then luckily, while the leader was searching my bag, he found out I was an aspiring Youth Corps member. He angrily threw my bag at me, and I remember him saying to his gang members, "This will teach him a very good lesson, bloody faggot."

The journey was to the mountain. Homosexuality will never be eliminated, but what about eliminating homophobia? On January 7, 2014, in the secret of the Aso Rock villa—the office and official residence of the president of Nigeria—Pres. Goodluck Jonathan signed the Same-Sex Marriage (Prohibition) Act of 2013. It was one of the most vicious and draconian pieces of legislation to come out of Nigeria and Africa in 2014. At the time, I was traveling to Abuja to attend one of the late-night parties usually organized in Abuja, the Federal Capital Territory. Before the law was passed, Abuja used to be the hub of our parties, a city with diplomatic representatives and beautiful lighting. I call it the New York City of Nigeria, and it held the power of the entire nation. But the tragedy that befell gay men started on that day. The tension that came with this law proved that gay life in Nigeria was going to be condemned.

The truth remains. I love my home country, the pride of West Africa and also known as the giant of Africa. I am proud of it and the joy that comes in our struggles and resilience, the brilliance in our craft and creativity, and our pride in remarkable figures, just like my childhood role model—Fela Anikulapo Kuti, the man who spoke the truth through music.

A great artist and activist for humanity, Kuti criticized the corruption of Nigerian government officials and the mistreatment of Nigerian citizens. He spoke of colonialism as the root of the socioeconomic and political problems that plagued the African people. Corruption was one of the worst, if not the worst, political problems facing Africa in the 70s, and Nigeria was among the most corrupt countries of the time. The Nigerian government was responsible for election rigging and coups that ultimately worsened poverty, economic inequality, unemployment, and political instability, which further promulgated corruption and thuggery. Fela's protest songs covered themes inspired by the realities of corruption and socioeconomic inequality in Africa. Fela Kuti's political statements could be heard throughout Africa. Little did I know that my own life was going to be fashioned by his songs, which I had listened to as a child.

I have lived my adult life with a focus of helping to create a world where people can live full and happy lives and allowed them their inherent human characteristics. The life-threatening conditions in my home country have forced me to seek an asylum in the United States. I miss the food my mother prepares to celebrate the New Year, my native dish Ukodo, which is made from yam, plantains, fresh fishes, and hot spices. I miss the warm tropical rain forest, the beautiful coconut trees, and the salt- and freshwater fish. I know for sure I am going to miss my friends, the night parties we go to, and the opportunity to wear clothes to express gender identity, celebrate drag, and hide and seek romance. Yes, my expectations are high, but are we constantly going to flee persecution? What has happened to the power of protest and resistance that was shown by our heroes of 1960, the men and women who said "Enough is enough. Let's take our freedom back"? Now we are even suffering more in the hands of our government than we did under colonization, but as Fela Kuti sang, "My people are suffering and smiling, pushing young people to trade the beautiful rain forest, mangrove savanna, and beautiful desert for hurricanes, cold temperatures, and racial indifference."

Two weeks after the law was passed, the dark days fell upon us, on the Gishiri community in Abuja that was a safe haven to many LGBTQ. These lovely people have had to find refuge, solace, and support in the arms of their brothers and sisters. The new reality of Nigeria that began is that it is now life-threatening to associate with any sexual orientation that is not heterosexual.

Government and private citizens now blame the LGBTQ for all the woes in Nigeria. We are scapegoats with no safe haven. Some stories I have heard include the following:

The Gishiri community was invaded. The day of remembrance dawned on the LGBTQ haven in the Gishiri community. These men broke into the neighborhood that housed more than forty-plus suspected gay men in Abuja, inspecting the houses one after the other, dragging out the men found in the rooms. The initial plans were to cleanse the land by killing the homosexual men and use their blood to cleanse the community for the curse they have brought to the community. Policemen were standing behind the invaders and watching the humiliation and dehumanizing treatment and did not respond. The whole time, the invaders were shouting, "We are carrying out the president's orders, 'kill the gays' bill!" The Same Sex Marriage Prohibition Act (SSMPA) has changed the climate of the country, and invaders are now using this opportunity to practice jungle justice. The invaders used hoes and cutlasses, as well as large pieces of wood studded with sharp nails and other metallic weapons, to flog the suspected gay men. At the end of the day, you could not recognize the faces of the men who have suffered beatings from the invaders. Then they were asked to leave the community and never return or face the ultimate penalty of death. Where do you want someone who has been rejected by family and friends to go? This gave birth to the walk of shame. Thousands have fled home as a result of this law. Oh, Mother Nigeria, why treat your children differently?

The party I was going to attend in Abuja had been canceled because news traveled so fast that any gathering would spark the same treatment from the hands of the angry Nigerians who had taken the law into their hands.

I could not sleep that night; my fear and anxiety grew that one day this would be my fate. Abuja, which I used to describe to my friends both at home and abroad as the gay capital of West Africa, has now become a land of horror.

On February 6, barely a month after the law was passed and two weeks after the horrible situation in the Gishiri community, another horror broke out in Gwagwalada, Abuja. I was prepared to attend this particular event with my friends in Abuja. In advance, we have discussed how we would express ourselves, and my friend even told me how "Gwarinpa girls" would dominate the party. But before our arrival, the police had displayed their magical show. The police were tipped off by an unknown person who had gotten information of the location where the gathering was going to take place. The police came with the information that there was going to be a gathering of gay men in Gwagwalada. Before the law, such parties took place without any disturbance from the police and community. These parties where the only opportunity for LGBTQ persons to express themselves. Before the law, such parties would happen frequently with no consequences. Now the law in full effect had empowered homophobic people.

The police came to the location barely before the party began and arrested the guys who were present and falsely claimed they were planning to do a gay wedding. They took the men to the police station and asked them to pay for their release. I was lucky I had not yet gotten to the party, as I would not have been able to pay the bond. Hearing what had happened sent more chills up my spine. I asked myself that if this massacre was happening in Abuja, how much worse must it be in eastern Nigeria where I had attended school in Enugu state and which had and still has a bad reputation for notorious kidnapping, extortion, and blackmail? This law had opened the doors for thugs as it became a business for the thugs to extort and blackmail gay men.

In quick succession, there were raids by police. They regularly and routinely arrested members of the gay community and approached various people for bail. This extortion continued. On one specific time, they raided the only health-care center providing HIV and STI services for gay men in Garki, Abuja. The executive director of the organization at this time was celebrating his birthday, and there was a large gathering of men drinking and partying. The police arrived with the environmental protection board, with the intention of persecuting the men they would find. The police started with a search of the entire office and found no incriminating property or suspected activity of homosexual practice. Of course, they would not find anything since the center was a clinic that provided medical services and legal protection for the LGBT community. The police took and detained the executive director, but he was released after a few hours of interrogation.

This resulted in the first lawsuit against the Nigerian police; the executive director filed a lawsuit against the Nigerian police and the environmental protection board. This was the first break of daylight for the community stripped of its basic human rights. This act of bravery encouraged young LGBT community members and international bodies, but despite this lawsuit, the vicious attacks on innocent community members continued in full force.

Spring of the same year, there was an attack against a community member in Durumi, Abuja. This attack was one of the most life-threatening attacks I have seen before my own persecution. The victim was called Ijeoma in the community—a guy answering to a female name since Ijeoma was a name for women mostly from southeastern Nigeria and the northern parts of Delta State, my state of origin—because of his looks. There was a stereotypical attribute to feminine behavior in Nigeria that only gays gesticulate, and masculinity was promoted by the culture, indirectly making women lesser than men by the interpretation of West African tradition. Ijeoma lived with a guy, and both of them worked as peer educators for the center. They did HIV education and usually carried condoms and lubricants in their bags to give to community members who did not have access. On their way from a peer education program, they were caught by a mob who had suspected Ijeoma of being gay. When they searched his bag and found condoms and lubricants, that was the end of the discussion as that was enough proof that he was gay. Then the screaming people gathered around them, and the treatment that was given to them was far, far worse than what a murderer or thief that was caught in the community would face. They were beaten up with all types of metallic objects and stripped naked. Tin cups threaded with ropes were tied to their waists. Children, mothers, grandparents, and community advocates for the end of gay existence sang songs, flogging them with horse whips and chanting, "We are carrying out Jonathan's law, 'jail the gay' bill." The police arrived and made the situation worse by bench-watching this dehumanizing activity and doing nothing. The men were tied inside a room, and the crowd threatened to burn them alive with petrol and matchsticks when the same group of men who came with the district police officers (DPO) asked them to stop and took them to the police station.

My people have been suffering from these attacks. Do you judge my actions and tell me that I was a fool to stand up for what was right with all these punishments? You call me a fool for losing my nationality. You ask me to be quiet and remain in a country that refuses to give equal protection to its citizens. Do you think Nigeria deserves to house humans when it has such an inhumane law?

THE ROLE OF OBAMA AND THE RESPONSE BY NIGERIAN LEADERS AND THE PRESS

Response by President Obama

Obama issued a memo ordering American diplomats abroad to advance the rights of lesbian, gay, bisexual, and transgender persons. The US government also announced that the fight against gay and lesbian discrimination would be a central point of its foreign policy, and transgressing nations like Nigeria could be denied aid.

Response by the Nigerian press to Obama's threat

On Obama's threat, the Nigerian press, particularly Zakari Mohammed, a Nigerian lawmaker, said, "We have a culture. We have religious beliefs and we have a tradition. We are black people. We are not white, and so the US cannot impose its culture on us. Same sex marriage is alien to our culture and we can never give it a chance. So, if [Western nations] withhold their aid to us, to hell with them."

Comment by the Nigerian senate president David Mark when passing the bill

"No country has the right to interfere in the way we make our own laws because we don't interfere in the way others make their own laws."

What the country's minister for information Labaran Maku said during a press conference

"Between Europe, America and Africa there is a huge culture gap. Some of the things that are considered fundamental rights abroad also can be very offensive to African culture and tradition and to the way we live our lives here."

Reuben Abati, presidential spokesman, said, "More than 90 percent of Nigerians are opposed to same-sex marriage. So, the law is in line with our cultural and religious beliefs as a people."

International condemnation by media

Amnesty International urged Jonathan to reject the bill, calling it "discriminatory" and warning of "catastrophic" consequences for Nigeria's lesbian, gay, bisexual, and transgender community.

Leading Nigerian authors' condemnation

Leading authors including Chimamanda Ngozi Adichie and Jackie Kay have condemned Nigeria's harsh, new antigay law in the strongest possible terms, with Kay comparing the situation to Nazi Germany and Adichie calling for the "unjust" law to be repealed.

Award-winning author Bernardine Evaristo added her voice to the chorus of writers protesting the legislation. "As someone with a Nigerian father I am particularly incensed by Nigeria's recent anti-gay legislation, but also the terrible increase in persecution of homosexuals across the African continent," she said. "The way in which both church and state are now inciting homophobic hatred to curry favour with their constituencies is abhorrent to me. It's just plain backwards when in some parts of the world many nations are moving forwards in their acceptance of homosexuality."

Nigerian novelist Helon Habila, winner of the 2001 Caine Prize, criticized Nigeria's government. "It is clear this is a government which is short of ideas, desperately trying to bring up nonsensical diversions to distract attention from the situation in the country. Just yesterday there was the attack on the boarding school. This government has lost the war on terror. So what they have decided to do is start inventing laws against gays, just to get the support of the people," he said.

"That is so wrong, and so sad. Instead of talking about the $20bn [£12bn] which is missing, they are happy to persecute gays, to stone them, in some places, and to harass them. It is just public entertainment the government is giving the people, like the Romans having gladiators to satisfy the people. It shows their bankruptcy of ideas, it is just desperation from the government, and people are dying because of it, are unnecessarily suffering because of it."

CHAPTER TWO

My Escape

The part of Africa where I grew up, like many other societies in West and North Africa, accepts heterosexism as a norm, and this belief has increased the expectation of parents that every guy at a particular age should be prepared for or have children. Institutionalized homophobia is standard practice in this part of the world, just as in eighty-plus countries where it is illegal to be gay, where the media is perpetuating stereotypes. Without having an all-inclusive antidiscriminatory bill, these countries transcend into far more overbearing interpersonal homophobia that leads to internalized homophobia expressed by homophobic people against other persons that are open to being themselves.

In 2016, I was employed by a community-based organization that advocated for gay men to have access to health-care service in Abuja, Nigeria. I chose to do the work of advocacy over my degree after I had spent five years studying to become a food scientist because I envisioned a country that would support its citizens, protect their basic human rights, and treat them equally. My friends and people I know were dying from unknown diseases, and most of them were afraid to approach the health-care providers because of discrimination, so I decided to be a voice for the people and join an organization that stands by the people affected. Although this facility provided treatment for sexual minorities, people were afraid to access these services because of stigma and internalized homophobia. My choice to join this organization was solely because of my passion and drive to support the LGBT community.

Most gay rights activists had run from Nigeria at this time. People who were educated about the issue were constantly being attacked, and they fled to Europe and North America. It became more and more obvious that I would be of immense help to the gay community by providing peer education and also sexual education, condoms, and legal education for a marginalized minority community. After the law was passed, there was an exponential increase in the prevalence of HIV among gay men in Nigeria.

My love for Nigeria and the fact that I have to stay and help my community could not override my personal safety. I wished I could have a stable relationship, be free, and not be in a state of constant fear of what might happen next. With widespread sentiment, the saying "There is no place like home" still remained. I wanted to leave the country for fear of being caught again and suffering mob attacks, but I did not know where to go. While I wanted to live freely, I was going to miss the fear, rejection, and pain, which had become part of my existence so far. Leaving it behind and moving on became very difficult since I knew no other life.

The year before, in 2015, I was fed up with Nigeria and wanted to escape, and it was my very first attempt to run away from Nigeria. I left for Accra, Ghana, in July of 2015 and landed in the city center by 11:00 p.m. I had little money, so I took a bus ride from Abuja to Lagos and left from Lagos. It was an eight-hour ride with stops in the Benin Republic and Togo. I was welcomed by my gay friend Kwesi. Kwesi had a masters in petroleum engineering from London (United Kingdom), and he was older than me and understood the Ghana gay community very well. He had told me of a party that he was invited to in Labadi Beach, Accra, but he first took me to a Ghanaian *mama-put*. This is a roadside restaurant, where the owner of the mama-put was the waitress, preparer of the food, and personal accountant. Here, we had the best of the best local Accra dish—kenkey and fish. When we were done with the local dish, we took a car rental service to the party.

When we got to the party that was held on Labadi Beach, we were welcomed by fresh breezes from the ocean surrounded by palm trees and nice Afro-beat sounds from every corner of the beach. I was drawn to the Nigerian DJ and carried away by the variety of DJs from different parts of West Africa and the mix of gay, lesbians, bisexuals, transgenders, and straight allies who all danced to the Ghana Azonto dance beats. It was the balm, a celebration of life. This was how I spent my first night in Accra.

The next morning, I woke up excited that I had finally escaped from the hands of horror in Nigeria. When my friend woke up and came to my room, I started narrating the beauty of the night that had just passed—how I danced, how joy overcame my pains. He took time to say something, and then I was confused.

"Kwesi, what is the problem?" I asked. He told me of his experience as a gay man who had crossed the thirty-year age bracket and had a master's from abroad, but there was still the expectation from his family for him to have a girlfriend or at least have a child. Ghana was not more accepting of homosexuality, and I would realize this soon. The benefit of the night we enjoyed was entirely due to the large sum of money paid to the police to stay calm and stay away for just one night.

I could only stay a week and soon realized there was little or no difference between living in Nigeria and living in Ghana. Here, too, the suffering of folks in Accra could be measurable to the life in Nigeria for gay men. In Ghana, people also get burned to death for being suspected to be gay and experience a "show" in the community called the walk of shame.

My friend Kwesi had called me recently, telling me of the life in Accra, how depressed he was, how he'd want to take his own life, and how he was looking for an opportunity to escape from Ghana.

ROLE OF NONGOVERNMENTAL ORGANIZATIONS AND ACTIVISTS

It was after I returned from my trip to Ghana that I undertook the job as a senior program officer in a community-based organization in Abuja, Nigeria, that provides access to health-care services for sexual minorities. I was always in the forefront of community dialogues, strategic committee meetings, and advocacy efforts to support our ongoing health education activities for men who have sex with men (MSM)—the legal term used by nongovernmental organizations to protect gay men so they could have access to treatment from the federal government. The sole reason I feel this program was accepted was because of the fund that the government got from the donors who provide funds to NGOs in country.

There were key roles played by NGOs in the Nigerian community, especially MSM-specific ones, such as community-based organizations. They provided litigation for MSM, documented abuses against gay men that were reported after the law was passed, and tried to provide health education and STI treatments and health-care access for HIV-positive folks. The report put together by a community-based organization in Lagos, Nigeria, in December 2015, entitled "Human Rights Violation Report," gave a perspective on the documented human rights abuses against gay men after the law was passed. These were markers that the law had caused more harm than good.

Health-care providers discriminated suspected gay men. A discriminatory statement used by a lady nurse to my friend made him refuse to see any health-care provider. This continuous discrimination drastically reduced the number of sick gay men seeing a health-care provider.

In the case of my friend, he went to the general hospital in Garki because he was ill and I had asked him to seek the assistance of a well-trained medical personnel. He yielded to my advice and visited the clinic, but when I called him later that same day, he was crying on the phone and explained to me how the nurse there had called him a faggot and claimed that only gay men get sexually transmitted diseases. She told him that he should be ashamed of himself walking like a sissy. I owed him the responsibility of comforting him because I had recommended he see a doctor, and now I had become the bad person who had placed my friend on the path of being less mentally stable. He continued crying on the phone, and I already knew what my next response would be—to march to that hospital and complain to the nurses' office. But instead, I remained calm and supported my friend who felt helpless.

When my friend dropped the call, reality dawned on me that this could have been someone else who did not have someone to speak with. This is just one of the many cases that go undocumented, and nobody cared about the welfare of people.

THE ATTACK THAT ALMOST TOOK MY LIFE

Summer of 2016, I was finally in a relationship for the first time and was happy with the opportunity I had because I could express my emotions with someone. I was beginning to understand and grow as a person. Since I was living in a society that did not allow such kind of relationship between two men, I tried to manage this secret relationship by reducing the amount of time we met. When he called me, I had to run from everybody to pick up the call because I didn't want people around me asking why I was speaking so softly in this very noisy society.

I was barely a few months into this relationship when I suffered a mob attack. That night in July, I had gone to a club in Wuse 2, Abuja. Wuse was known for its nightlife, characterized by its signature clubs and women and men prostitutes standing on the streets at night, shielded by dim streetlights. Wuse had undeniably one of the best nightlife districts in the country. Some of my friends and I, including the guy I was dating, decided to go clubbing. We took a car rental service since no one wanted to drink and drive and we had planned to drink as much as we could that night. I usually celebrate my birthday on July 23 of every year, and it was a plus that the date was actually a Saturday night. We started with a bar in Wuse, stayed up till midnight, and moved to a club to dance and wind to the Afro beats.

While we were dancing, I was reflecting on the past years and the sufferings the gay community had suffered. In the bar where we were drinking, one of my friend who was dancing came back and told us that the guys across us were looking at us and were gossiping that we must be gay guys, hanging out together with no ladies. So the club would be safer since it was crowded, and my friends could tell I was one of the most passionate Nigerian dancers. I liked the Afro-beat sounds of Nigerian musicians, which was one of the reasons why my love for Nigeria was never-ending. I could not stop dancing at the club that night, but everything that has a beginning also has an ending, so the night came to an end by 3:00 or 4:00 a.m. in the morning.

"I don't want to go home," I said to my friends. It was hard to stop that moment when you feel light and unburdened because it only comes once in a blue moon in Nigeria. The political climate was so bad for gay men. They were not able to gather in a bar and spend time without being targeted by a mob. My friends called me a car rental service that took me home that night, and I did not know how I had gotten home—drunk and happy.

The sleep I was having ended when I heard the chant in front of my door while I was in my bed. The storm blew in with wild thunder; the community mob of Durum was at my front door, chanting, "He's gay. We have found out. We would kill him and use his blood as a sacrifice to cleanse the community. He is advocating against our belief [religious belief, both Christian and Muslim], and the law of our land demands he must be killed. His witchcraft has left our community with misery."

How quickly the drum had changed its beating—from dancing to the Afro beats in the club last night to dancing to the masqueraded and mob beats of the Durumi community in the morning. I remained quiet inside my room, wondering what had led to this kind of chant. The community had been targeting me before, but no one had approached me before. I suspected the lady who asked me why I always carried a unisex bag. She was fearless to ask me "Are you gay?" but I did not respond to her. The fear I had of being mobbed had now become a reality. I had wanted to relocate, but now the mob had caught up with me a few days before I could relocate to safety.

The mob broke into my silence and caught me in the middle of my thoughts as to what to do or how to escape. I knew I could not call the police because they were the number one perpetrators of violence against gay men. The police in Nigeria even stop people and search their phone and bags to find any reasons to arrest them as gays.

The mob broke my door with one push from three to four heavy men, and I had no place to hide in my room. I was still only wearing shorts and had no shirt on when I returned from the club. I had taken off my outside clothes and could not shower or wear nightclothes. The men gripped me by my wrist and dragged me out of my house, but I could not scream. I knew no one would help me because they were all on the same side.

People where prepared outside with machetes and horse whips, and children were clapping and singing after me. That was all I knew before I blacked out, following a punch to my forehead. The next time I woke up, I was being caressed by a nurse. I had suffered from severe injuries and fractures on my body. My forehead had a huge open scar. There were also other scars and marks, which are still on my body and remind me of that day.

"Enough is enough," I said to myself. I could not continue to stay in this country and fight for survival and carry the burden of others and not preserve my life. This was when my escape journey started.

UAE EXPERIENCE

I had to leave Nigeria because the community members were after me, and the next time they get ahold of me, they were not going to have mercy on me because my friend told me that the crowd that night had left me in the gutter when I fainted and that they thought I was dead.

I applied for the United Arab Emirates and for a Dubai visa. I was able to get this Dubai visa very easily, compared to trying to get one for Europe and North America. Once I realized I had to leave, where I would go did not matter at the time. Life in Nigeria had become a daylight horror, and I felt like committing suicide. I had no options. I also felt embarrassed.

My friends told me that Dubai was a nice place to visit; however, I could not enjoy my stay in Dubai. I was worried as to what the outcome of my life would be. My friends in Abuja told me not to return, that the mob had sent a spy to know if I was still coming to work. At the same time, I could not stay in Dubai because they also don't accept gay people and were the extremes of Abuja. Also, I did not have papers to stay for more than two weeks in Dubai, and my primary reason for immigration had been to live freely as a gay man.

If this was my reason, I realized then that migration to Dubai was not the place for me, so I prepared and returned to Nigeria.

THE NIGHT IN CAIRO

I returned to Nigeria and resigned from my job in the community-based organization, then I started looking for a way to flee Nigeria. When I got the invitation to come for a conference in the United States, I applied for a United States visa, and I also got an invitation to speak in France at the Open Government Partnership (OGP) conference in December 2016. I was very intrigued by the opportunities presented before me. Although I got my US visa in early October 2016, I remained in Nigeria even after getting the visa to flee the country. Who in his right mind, when presented the opportunity, would not flee since he had been suffering from mob violence? However, my love for the gay community and the country stopped me from leaving, so I continued my work. In late October 2016, my name and photographs were published as a recipient of the Falobi Award for grassroots advocacy for men who have sex with men (MSM) in Nigeria, and this award and publicity made me a more prominent target by the Durumi community members who had previously thought I had died as a result of the beatings I suffered in July. Now my life was in more imminent danger, so I got a flight ticket and flew to Cairo, Egypt. I had been persecuted in the past and feared nearly to death what would happen this time if I was caught by the mob in Abuja, Nigeria.

When I got to the airport in Abuja to fly to Cairo, I started crying because I knew I had more to give to my country, but I could do no more. I could do no more than protect my life and use the cash I had to take me anywhere. When I got to Cairo, the climate had changed. My journey as a refugee had begun; I had lost my home and was now externally displaced. I stayed in a hotel that night, and the night was longer than usual as I wept, asking myself what I could do next, where I would stay.

If I had the power to turn back the hands of time, I wondered, what would I have done differently? But this would not solve my problem of homelessness, which left my limited options wide open: will I fly to the United States, which I had a visa for, or return to Nigeria and face more persecution? I could not find a solution to the questions popping in my head. *Where will I stay? How will I eat?*

I left the room so I won't harm myself and walked to the pool area where I saw people sitting with their families and smiling. I lit a cigarette and smoked away my anxiety and fear. I said to myself, *Desperate times demand desperate measures.* I sat on the swing close to the pool and napped for a few minutes until the waitress came and woke me up to go inside my room because it was late. I could not tell her how worried I was or how I needed someone to speak with.

Walking toward my room, I picked up my phone and texted four of my friends back home that I might not return to Nigeria, and I texted my colleagues who had traveled to the United States on Facebook that they might see me soon in New York. My fear of being homeless had prompted me to start messaging random people on Facebook who were Africans and Nigerians who lived in the New York area because my flight would land in JFK. It took me a sleepless night to realize I had no friend or family currently living in the United States.

Letter of Lamentation of a Friend

I am worried about how to rebuild my life; the journey is *long*! Even after I adjust my immigration status, I have to figure out a career path etc. It's a long, hard, painful journey but am committed to the end! But no regrets! Nigeria has nothing to offer me anymore.

CJ

This piece was written to me by a friend who recently immigrated to the United States, lamenting, explaining, and expressing the difficulty, fears, and pain it took to lose his home, his career, and the life he grew up to understand. He also lamented his immigration status, which required documentation from time to time, and also expressed the fear of changing his career and how he hoped to be strong and resilient. The future was uncertain, but he was ready to hold on; he was afraid but had no regrets. A living thing is better than a dead sacrifice.

These and many more were the cries of asylum seekers who lost their lives because of their sexuality and who were able to defeat the trials and defeat the past and move on. Being reminded of the hurts of their past was opening sores that were trying to heal.

CHAPTER THREE

Bed 26

Life is a miracle, and every breath we take is a gift. I woke up this morning with a different aura, but my morning ritual would not change because I found myself in a strange room—the strangest room I have ever been in. I got down on my knees to say a word of gratitude, for I could not be more grateful to see another day. Then while I was down on my knees, I heard the officer shouting, "Wake up, you all. Wake up, guys! Breakfast is served."

I was filled with disbelief and continued asking myself, "Where am I?" It was the question I have yet to find an answer to this day.

A French-speaking guy greeted me, "Bonjour, Bed 26." I assumed he believed I was from West Africa or Asia, and now my new name was Bed 26. I was wondering. While he called me Bed 26, others approached me and called me the same name. Then he walked me to the dining table section of our room—my new home. The dining section was just in front of the television, and the guys in the room were watching an ABC morning news show. I was bluntly quiet, listening to the conversation of the two guys from Tanzania that I joined at the table and my new friend, the French guy, who was from Burkina Faso.

The Tanzanian guy was the first to ask me. "What brought you here?"

I replied to him, "Last night I was brought here by two officers who dropped me off at the front desk, and a lady entered my details into a database with a very large computer that was made in the eighties. Then she gave me a blue hand band that had my bed number, 26, and my alien number, with a head-shot photo that was taken with me wearing a blue jumpsuit and a white T-shirt. This kit was given to me as my new clothes.

My little bags and the property I came with were traded for these clothes. I am now wearing clothes that no one would wish to wear."

They started laughing so hard, and the French guy told me he had been there for over nine months. He lost his case and was now waiting for the appeal. The Tanzanian guys had met on the plane on their way to the United States, and they had just arrived a few nights before me.

We all did not discuss for long because shortly after breakfast, it would be count time. We had to return to our bed and wait to be counted like chickens, but before we left the table, the guys told me that most of the people here had never done any crime. They were all fleeing persecutions from their home countries.

I remembered my own situation. A few days before, I was in my home country, Nigeria, living in fear and hiding from the attack I was likely to face as a human rights activist. I thought my life was coming to an end because of the belief that people like me, gays, do not deserve to be human. The Nigerians who threatened me thought that homosexuality was against the culture and belief of West African tradition and "the culture of my people." As a result, I had suffered from many discordant relationships, lack of acceptance from my family, and rejection from friends and the community. Most of the time, I had lived in pretense in order to keep some of the relationships in my lifetime because of my work and to prevent the backlash from my community. But I was very stubborn.

I had always stood for what was right and what I believed in. There was a saying, and I lived with this idea: "Belief is stronger than tens of thousands of armies"—despite a national law that criminalized same-sex relationships and punished anybody that provided safe haven for people who were engaged in same-sex sexual activity in Nigeria. I was only going to hide for a while before my persecutors caught up with me and likely stone me to death by Sharia law and/or I would be given fourteen years of jail term by the federal law.

I got to my bed for count, lay in my bed facing the roof, and imagined the room of forty-four guys all sleeping in flat bunk beds, wearing the same blue jumpsuit and white T-shirt. The maximum occupancy of my room was forty-four, and we were filled to capacity with people from different parts of the world all stuffed together in a small room among many other rooms. Some occupants in other rooms were wearing orange jumpsuits. As I was wondering what I had gotten myself into, in my head, I realized I had seen such uniforms before when I watched the American series *Prison Break*.

I was in jail, but it was a special type of jail called detention and was for housing immigrants who crossed the border without appropriate documents, had expired visas, had overstayed their visas, had been deported before, or were caught by immigration officers (ICE) for doing little or no crime, like drinking and driving. What had brought a man running for his dear life into a jail? I had a visa; I had never been to the States before. Was that the best way to welcome an immigrant?

MY LIFE AND NIGERIA'S BACKGROUND

Where I Started

Let me go back to the beginning.

My name is Nong Richie. I am from Warri, Delta State, Nigeria. Before Nigeria gained independence from Britain in 1960, there had been tensions between the diverse ethnic groups and the leadership of the country. As the second most important oil-producing city in Nigeria after Port Harcourt, Warri, Delta State, was claimed as homeland by three major ethnic groups: the Itsekiri, the Urhobo, and the Ijaw. I am an Urhobo man by ethnicity, and this group dominated most of the local governments of Delta State.

One source summarized: "The Niger Delta is home to some forty different ethnic groups dispersed in 3000 or so communities, with a total population variously estimated at 20–40 million people and housed in nine federating states: Rivers state, Abia, Awka-Ibom, Bayelsa, Ondo, Cross River, Delta, Edo and Imo. Niger's Delta are the highest producer of crude oil, Nigeria major source of economic survival and natural resource sustaining an estimated 185 million people ranked among the 8 largest population in the world."

Warri happens to be my city of birth and is the largest town (though not the capital) of Delta State. Here you would find good aquatic farms surrounded by a large body of water and arable land used in growing root crops like cassava and large tubers of cocoyams, despite the fact that they are one of the highest producers of petroleum and are the home to state-of-the-art refinery (Effurun refinery). Warri is nicknamed the Oil City and had been home for years to large oil corporations, like Shell, ExxonMobil, and Agip. However, Warri still finds herself in the situation of violent despair and poverty, which is characterized by bad roads that cause loss of harvested agricultural products through the transportation chain, inflation of food prices, poor health-care systems, and mismanagement of existing structures.

I remember the days when I was much younger, watching the news and always hearing of fire explosions from one to another, fuel pipeline leakages, pollution of the bodies of water, and oil spillages killing sea animals and destroying the arable farmlands. This constant pollution affected the economy and welfare of the Niger Delta, had increased the fragility, and exposed the elderly, children, and young ones to dangerous conditions and high fatality rates. Sadly, the survival of the fittest, Charles Darwin's theory of evolution, became the order of survival for people with the most priced asset, the nation's number one natural resource—not it people but its oil.

The constant leakage of fuel pipelines led to a mass upheaval as streets were occupied by angry people and protesters and riots struck from every part of the city. My people were tired of the government and how they milked their lands and did not support development and growth.

In May 1999, there seemed to be a new dawn for Nigeria when Olusegun Obasanjo took office as the president of Nigeria, ending multiple decades of military rule that began in 1966 and had been interrupted only by a brief period of democracy from 1979 to 1983. This was the era of massive corruption, which spelled doom for the Niger Delta region of Nigeria— exporting crude oil, which was valuable at this time; using the resource in developing properties outside the country in places like London and Dubai; and growing wealth, leaving my people in a state of confusion. Retaliation from my people was to be involved in militant and violent groups to bring the government's attention to the issues they were faced with. I personally do not believe it was the best way to go about, mediating peace, but who am I to judge when I always protest the government policies when it becomes oppressive? Delta State, which produces 40 percent of Nigeria's oil and receives 13 percent of the revenue from production in the state, had a particularly controversial division of political and government positions and structures, over which representatives of different ethnic groups were struggling to find just representation and provide administration and leadership. Finally, the corruption and mismanagement in government that had left the region—from which Nigeria derived its wealth—poor and underdeveloped had created a large class of young men who had no hope of legitimate work that would fulfill their ambitions of being wealthy and successful. Such a group easily gave in to recruitment in violent groups, such as politicians and militants.

It was the period during the spring of confusion in the early 2000s that would define my educational career and provide the parenting opportunity offered to me by my aunt. I was born into a family of two sisters and one brother, with my father and mother alive and strong. My elder sister was celebrating her birthday, and I can vividly remember she was born on May 21. However, this day marked the misery of the new millennium for the people of Warri. While people were celebrating the crossover into the new millennium, the celebration only lasted for a few months before the tribal tension escalated into a war on that very night of May 21 in the year 2000. The sky was red at dusk, and usually, it was time to go to bed, but we were impatiently waiting for my elder sister to return from her birthday celebration. It was all to no avail, for our prayers for her to return home could not stop the raging people from the ethnic backlash once the fight began among the Urhobos, Ijaws, and Itshekiris, the three major ethnic groups sharing the landscape of Warri, Delta State. The drum of war had begun, and when the beat was playing, you could not stop the people from dancing. There is a saying, "You cannot beat a child and tell him not to cry." Likewise, the people of Warri were charged to take what they believed they truly deserve from the government—good roads, clean water, good schools, and democratic, transparent governance.

I was ten years old when the war was taking place. My mother, who was shivering and scared by the entire situation, asked me to hide under the bed. This was the traditional way of survival; whenever there was a war, a child would lie under the bed with their stomachs flat. It would prevent you from being hit by a flying bullet. I was under the bed for hours. When I heard a sound of jubilation, I ran out to join the celebration, but my mom's first response was to rebuke me to go back to my hiding place. *Why am I the only one who deserves to lie under the bed?* I was wondering. *It is because she loves me so much and doesn't want to lose me.* She told me of the death of a child she gave birth to in 1993 by cesarean section, a breech baby, and how since then I was her treasure—the last card, as she usually called me.

I soon understood from the faces I saw that my elder sister had returned home from her birthday celebration, but she was looking miserable. With her hair scattered, no shoes on her legs, her eyes very weak, her breath panting, she was narrating the story of how her party was destroyed. The fear she had was basically due to the response of the people in her party to the war: instant panic attacks, people clashing against one another as they ran up and down (cachous). When she came under the bed to see how I was doing, I asked her why she stayed late and made us all afraid. She said she was also afraid of being hit by a flying bullet, but she left because of the fear that the war would get to the partygoers and said that the invaders were not Urhobos. If they had caught her, they would shoot her flat dead. She explained that when she peeped outside of the hall where the party was taking place, she could vividly see the houses of people being set ablaze. People identified themselves by placing a mark in front of their doors. Just like the Passover feast in the Bible, you had to put the name of your ethnic group on the door so that people from your tribe could protect you.

The night was long, and my family was unsettled. Before I fell asleep, I asked my sister, "What is the cause of this war?"

She replied, "The people are tired of working like a monkey climbing up the tree to get food and for the baboon waiting to eat from their hard work."

I said, "I do not understand what you mean."

She smiled with unrest in her smile. "You cannot understand, my brother. When you grow up, you will find out for yourself. Just try to sleep. It is late to discuss the cause of the fighting."

Then the governor of the state, James Ibori, an Urhobo man who was also preserved as a member of the corruption caucus with the federal government, declared a curfew. There was to be no movement from 6:00 p.m. to 6:00 a.m. as a means to help subside the armed conflict and reduce the tension. Armed forces men were sent to the streets to keep the calm. All through the sleeping hours, the sound of gunshots were reduced to some bearable extent that would permit you to sleep as a child. The curfew was not obeyed by all members of the region, for others engaged in battle with the armed men, showcasing their powerful charms, trying to show that mechanically made bullets could not go through them. This was a pure display of black magic.

When the cocks crowed in the morning, I was woken up with a call. "Pack up our bags. We cannot live in Warri." At that moment, hundreds of people had died, and we were moving to a different city to join my dad's younger sister who lived in a city close enough to find peace and who had welcomed us to stay with them for a period of time till the war subsided. That was the first time I became internally displaced with my entire family, but I never knew what this meant as a child. We took as little as two bags, both held by my dad and elder brother, and walked through various police and military checkpoints. Since there was no form of transportation at this point, we had to walk more than ten miles to get transportation to my auntie's place. While we were walking to get transportation, we saw people on the floor who were shot dead. I became so tired and afraid my mom placed me on her back, and we continued. I slept on my mom's back. Even with the wild drum of war, the comfort and protection of an African mother was irreplaceable to a child.

The war continued and even grew bigger as the days went by. Shell Nigeria (SPDC) installations were taken over, leading to a drop in oil production. The House of Assembly decided to relocate the headquarters of the local government of Warri to Ogbe-Ijaw, a decision that brought relative peace back to the city.

The civil conflict subsided, and it was time to rebuild our lives. My parents returned to Warri with my elder brother and sister, leaving me and my immediate elder sister Sivweneta behind. My aunt was very educated—a lecturer at the Petroleum Training Institute (PTI), Effurun, the only petroleum institute in West Africa at that time, a position which proved how successful she was in academics. She was also a very good Christian. Both her prestigious characteristics as an academic and a Christian would shape any rotten mango, especially the Warri mentality I grew up in as a child.

My elder sister nicknamed herself Anita, but heaven knows where that name came from as we were told its meaning came from the spiritual marine world. The water goddess in my language is called *oghene rukuku*. They practice a religion called Igbe and give service to the river gods. Igbe tradition engages in a festival just before the raining season to bring back the rain from November, the dry season, to February. And rituals are performed during this festivity period by bringing materials such as goats, yams, plantains, and sodas to the river. As I had experienced as a child, when the practitioners believe you are possessed, they take you there for cleansing. This was our tradition before the white men came and brought us the Bible, which means Christianity was now practiced as a standard religion in southern Nigeria where the Niger Deltas were located.

Anita moved in with my mom's younger sister in Port Harcourt because of my aunt's husband, who always blamed her for his own misfortune. Port Harcourt city was located in Rivers State, which became the oil boom city after the civil conflicts. I was left with my aunt, a strong African woman as described by her peers. She had graduated from the great University of Benin, one of the first universities that was built in the Niger Delta region. Only great brains were admitted into the university back then because it was the only university in the region, and one national examination was written by aspiring college students. I could not even make it to Uniben when it was time for me to take my college entrance examination because I had been told from my childhood that one had to finish with distinction in six out of nine high school subjects to be admitted into this great college that was located in the ancient kingdom of Edo State, the house to the great oba of Benin Kingdom. The Benin Kingdom was well respected as a precolonial empire, which had dated back to the eleventh century CE until it was annexed by the British Empire.

Aunt Grace, whom I now know as a mother figure, envisioned a bright future ahead for me and was motivated to see me through college just like she did. She had been provided education by my father who had taken her in when she was a little girl after the death of their father. She was very intelligent, and no one would allow her to remain in my hometown, Egbo-Urhie, with no good education system. She always reminded me of how she came to the city and had to repeat four classes as the curriculum was different. She had found it difficult to accept the fate of repeating classes in the city, but in my tradition, the decision of the elders were yea and amen, with no further questioning. You must do it, or you drop out. She would shortly prove her critics wrong by blazing through her subjects with distinctions and graduating at the top of her class from the University of Benin in chemistry and now working as a lecturer to students studying welding and fabrication at the Petroleum Training Institute.

I admire her and have always wanted to be like her, successful according to the standards set—married, godly, and educated, she is the last child among three, the breadwinner, and the provider for her two elder brothers, including my dad, the eldest. She was the only one with a college degree in my family at this time. We usually describe her as a woman who had the strength of a lion. I enjoyed the benefits of her education, living with her as her son, for she was just married and had no child at this time. She schooled me and prepared me for my national examination to gain admission into high school, which is called secondary school in Nigeria. I did not have it easy going through this process, but she enrolled me for the federal government high school examination and prepared me day and night, waking me up to read at night. She took me to church every Sunday, and we would arrive before Bible study classes so I could memorize some Bible passages. She always read the Bible during our morning devotion and recited the passage to me, "Train up a child the way he should grow, and when he shall grow, he will never depart from it."

After the results of the national entrance examination into Federal Government College came, she drove me in her four-wheel drive white Toyota Sienna to school. Initially, I left disappointed because my name did not show up in the board. I was not admitted. I waited for the second batch, but still I was not admitted. I was bitter, angry at myself, and disappointed that now I was going to follow the footsteps of all my elder siblings who were not able to get a high school diploma or a higher degree.

My aunt did not stop our pursuit for me to start high school that year, and finally, in September 2002, my aunt asked me to go with her to the supermarket and told me that I would be starting secondary school. What a surprise! I questioned her because I was not given admission by FGC (Federal Government College), but she told me that I was given admission by Unity Model Secondary School, Agbarho. Jubilations would not stop for me. I jumped to my feet, happy that I was going to start a new life, leaving home and not having to deal with the constant nagging of my aunt's husband. I would be staying at the school hostel, which was compulsory for all new students.

Unity School, Agbarho, was the first high school in Bendel State then, which was part of the ancient Benin Empire, so I was proud of my future alma mater. I was also excited to be leaving home and no longer be policed police on what to do and what not to do or having to envy my neighbors' children who attended boarding schools and returned home with a lot of stories of how fun an experience they had living away from home. Of course, at the time, I did not know that being in boarding school came with many responsibilities, like washing my clothes myself, cleaning my bedsheets and making my bed in the morning, clearing the grass surrounding the hostel, sweeping the verandas and what have you, fetching water for senior students, and being flogged for coming late to the assembly or wearing a dirty sock. I wish I had been informed ahead of time that this decision was going to shape me and that it would not entirely be a jolly ride.

My aunt attended a good boarding school in her days, and one of my teachers was her classmate. Although she knew what I was going into, she said nothing and allowed me to find my way myself because she believed I was going to be shaped by the school system by following strict routines and activities, like military men and women—waking up at 5:00 a.m. with a bell, taking your shower and having breakfast before 6:30 a.m., joining the assembly line by 7:00 a.m., singing praise and worship, and reading the hymns from ancient and modern texts. All the routine we followed had been established by the British, and we followed this model because it has shaped a lot of graduates from the institution who were highly respected by society and who were also involved with the government and leadership of my state and the nation of Nigeria.

The people who called me Bed 26 understood and spoke Spanish and little English. At this detention center, the standard mode of identification was your bed number to both detainees and officers. It had been a system. The guards and staff of the detention center sneak people into the dormitory at night, and when the detainees wake up, they notice a new person in the room, so people try to become acquainted with you. I wanted to ask a question, but they understood only a little English, so I was quiet and somber. I had never been to a jail before, so in the beginning, I was trying to figure out a solution and questioned myself, *Is it not better if I die in Nigeria than to come and sit in prison in a different country?*

My new friend Jean from Burkina Faso asked me my name after count time.

I replied, "My name is Nong, and I am from Nigeria."

"Oh, my friend, there is a Nigerian in this room. I will show him to you, but he is currently in the kitchen, working," my new friend explained. In detention centers, detainees work in the kitchen between three daily shifts. Those in the morning shift leave very early, as early as 5:30 a.m. When the Nigerian had left for work that morning, I was still fast asleep. I had traveled twelve hours from Cairo to JFK nonstop, changing time zones, crossing the Atlantic Ocean from Africa to North America. I was happy that there were people of the same color and, somewhat, tradition as me. I had met an African, and there was another Nigerian I was going to meet later in the day.

I was housed in a detention center located in Elizabeth, New Jersey, a few steps from the Newark Liberty International Airport, surrounded by warehouses, with not one building to spare as the detention center itself was a former warehouse. It was covered in totality with not a single glimpse of the outside world. There were two square openings on the roof, directly on top of the dining chairs and tables, covered by a thick glass; the rooms were surrounded by high walls with just a little glass opening at the side where you could just see the sunrise and sunset. This was going to be my home for an unknown period. Bed 26 was the bunk bed close to the toilets and bathroom, which meant I was going to inhale people's waste since bathrooms were not properly cleaned due to poor cleaning supplies. All this meant I was in for the experience of a lifetime.

Jean asked me about my arrival to the States, "Did you not hear of the tension in America?"

I had arrived at JFK International Airport on October 28, 2016, a few days before the presidential election between Hilary Clinton and Donald Trump, and the political climate of the country was unsettling. This was not a good time for immigrants to arrive in a country that had previously had a virtue of upholding the inherent dignity of humankind. I was a novice, had never been to North America before, but from my youngest age, I had always known America to be the free world, a country that welcomed all. Now I was faced with a double trauma: fleeing persecution from my home country and arriving at an unsettling time. I held on to what I knew and believed in the justice system of America. Although none of my family members had ever traveled this far, I was a young man in a different world.

I had landed at JFK airport at about 3:15 p.m. and set off walking toward immigration to be checked in and to go into the world of freedom. The immigration officer stamped my passport and told me to enjoy my stay in America, at which point I walked up to the baggage claim area of the airport at terminal 4, picked up my bag, and did not know what to do next. I imagined how life would start in this new country, walked outside, and settled for a cigarette to help reduce my tension. I had no clue of what to do next, and I walked up to an immigration officer, explaining to him that I just arrived on a plane and I had come seeking freedom. He was very polite then and walked me to a private room and asked me to wait. He told me I would be attended to. This was the beginning of my journey to freedom. Deep inside, I felt safe and was happy. The room had a clear white painting. It was quiet, surrounding me with serenity. There was a table in front of me and a chair across and a glass of water on the table, and the cooling system was working fine.

I had landed in the land of dreams—America. The clock in front of me was ticking. I could hear the sound clearly as time was rolling on. A few minutes of waiting grew into hours, so I decided to rest my hand on the table and take a little nap. When I woke up and looked at the time, it was 6:20 p.m., yet no one had come to speak with me. After a few more minutes of waiting, a huge Asian-looking guy walked into the room and introduced himself. I wasn't interested in what he was going to say because I believed affluent people in America were all whites and I believed he was only a messenger, a prejudice I had grown up with. He asked me some few questions, like my name, where I am from, what brought me here, and why I could not return to my country. After rigorous questioning that lasted up to an hour, he left. Then he returned and asked me to go with him to search for my luggage. I had come with a bag that had pieces of papers. Just about every document I have had in my lifetime was in that luggage, dating back to my birth certificate. Then he asked me to return to the room.

I became afraid as I walked back to the room because I could not understand the reason for this questioning and checking. I had come here to ask for freedom. My fear was not just sentimental, however, for when I was walking back to the room, I saw people outside in the large room being held for questioning and a guy was handcuffed. The officer said I should wait and somebody would come and speak with me. The lady that I saw next with some papers asked me to read and sign a document stating that I could not return to my country. She read out to me that I would not be returned to my country as I was afraid of being returned to my country because of the persecution I was likely to face. Here in the US, I would be housed in a jail. My fear became a reality. *I am going to jail in America. There is no freedom for me anymore.*

The Asian officer asked me to come with him to another room where I was asked to hold a board like a criminal. Photos of me where taken, my measurements were also taken, and finally, I was asked to join a guy in a holding cell at the airport. The guy, who was facing deportation, explained to me what just happened based on his experience. Asylum seekers were treated like criminals at the borders; the officer would treat you more like a common thief or drug dealer caught crossing the border. They gave no consideration to someone fleeing their country and thus entitled to petition for freedom and safety in the United States.

My experience at Unity School, Agbarho, taught me to be competitive since the choices we made as students were determined by our performances at the various national examinations. For example, in the junior secondary school, examination students were classified based on their performance in sciences and arts, which determine their placement into appropriate classrooms that match their scores as science, social science, and art students. This system chose what was best for us and what we were to study in college, the same way the border patrol officers chose available housing for detainees. My school matched me according to my performance in junior secondary school. I wish the American immigration system could use my experience as someone who had suffered trauma and fought for others' freedom and grant me a stay outside the detention center. My fate was decided as a child to become a science student because of my performance in chemistry, physics, and biology and was against my wishes to study history and economics. However, I did not complain because I was proud of the feat I had achieved to be in science classes—a treasured position for millennials. My fate was also decided—to stay in a detention jail, an experience which I could never be proud of.

In my nuclear family, no child of my parent had gotten a high school diploma and successfully gained admission into college, but this spell ended with me. Now, in comparison, what is the difference between me and those who did not go to college when my degree had been placed as second best in a new society where I was being made to start with prison life? I knew how I suffered to gain admission into college because I believed the odds were against me. I secured admission into college on my first attempt, but I could not attend school in my home state because of the students in my high school days that would return to mock me based on my experience of being accused of being "a faggot." Subsequently, my mother had arranged with a friend of hers, and I was accepted into a predegree program at Enugu State University of Science and Technology in Enugu, Nigeria, hundreds of miles from my home state.

Stigma from childhood had affected my choice of schooling, but I studied hard during this program, and after nine months, I was accepted to a degree program to study food science and technology. When I returned home and told my friends that I had been accepted to study and become a food scientist, my friend in Warri laughed at me. "Others are studying petroleum and chemical engineering, but you study food science?" Because we were from the oil city, there were a lot of jobs in petrol chemicals, but not in food science and technology. At the same time, due to the civic unrest and other environmental struggles attributed to our environment, men were considered worthy to be called men only if they were very masculine and if they followed the norm of being engineers, doctors, or lawyers, which were considered masculine jobs worth spending hard-earned money to get training and degrees in. Thus, I was ashamed of myself, yet I could not believe the ridicule they gave me when I had expected them to celebrate the fact that I gained admission into college. My family members contributed and made comments that were also offensive, especially my immediate elder sister who called me a sissy and a waste of money and effort.

Finally, the spell of no one having a high school diploma in my family would be broken, but what is the difference between someone who studied food science and someone who did not go to school? That was the topic of discussion. My father who could not afford my school fees still had the guts to insult me by calling me "sissy." His ignorance came into play, but I was young and felt discouraged. As a result, I made the personal decision to study and make good grades and then to change my course of study in my second year of college to medicine as this would give me the gratification I deserved at the time, although my university had not been accredited for medicine. The course of studies would take me eight to nine years to complete. Then if it was not accredited at the time of my graduation, I had plan B to apply for another school or change to engineering.

Registering for courses in my second year, I discovered food science and chemical engineering where going to be doing the same course, so I had a change of mind and focused on competing with the engineering students as a means of proving to my peers that food science was not a course for women. I was doing all this to impress people and make them realize that I am a man as the masculinity norm that was instilled in me from childhood began to manifest. Warri guys always try to prove they are strong and rugged; their bodies are filled with marks from wounds made from bottles that look like designs of tattoos. Likewise, they are expected to abuse marijuana, alcohol, and other hard drugs. These and many more were the true identity that they use to define the mark of a Warri boy (masculinity).

My classmates criticized me for always studying and not displaying the rugged characteristic that had been identified in a Warri boy. They said in pidgin English, "You nor they behave like Warri boy." I don't drink; neither do I have many female partners. This pressure changed the way I attended to things, and peer pressure led me into joining a secret cult and having a girlfriend to show off—all in desperation to prove my masculinity. I liked men, but I could not confide in anyone because everyone around me wanted me to show the fake part of me, which I could only fake for a short period of time.

At the airport holding room, the officers came and placed handcuffs on my legs and hands as they would a common thief, then walked me to the bus. As I was walking toward the bus, people who had just landed and were at the exit terminal waiting for friends and family to pick them up looked at me with eyes full of pity, as if I were some drug dealer who was caught with his goods confiscated. Finally, I got to the bus and was thrown into the back, and the doors were slammed.

The bus started moving; it was very quiet, except for the radio that was playing. The lady officer who was the driver was not talking. It was likely that she was frustrated with her job schedule, working at night at 11:00 p.m. when people were sleeping or spending time with their partners. I could feel her anger; I don't know if it was her job or personal life that made her push me to move when my legs were manacled and we were walking to the bus. It was fall, and the temperature was cold and windy, especially for a man like me who has lived all his life in the tropical rain forest. I could feel the car moving, the tires hitting neatly on the tired road. I was half-asleep and half-awake when the lights from the George Washington Bridge flashed into my eyes. I became fully awake, saying goodbye to the beautiful lighting of New York City.

At this point, all I could think about was Rosa Louise McCauley Parks, the first lady of the civil rights and the mother of the freedom movement. Parks refused to obey the bus driver James F. Blake's order to give up her seat in the colored section to a white passenger after the whites-only section was filled. In Nigeria, I had resisted the government from taking away my civil rights, fought for the community, and asked that people's civil rights should be respected. This call for justice had led me to be treated like a criminal. I found that some people I was fighting for, people like myself, wished me death because of my courage. It resonated in my head. I was asking myself questions. Is the movement worth dying for—my passion to see an end to injustice and maltreatment for men who have sex with other men (MSM) in Nigeria, which has the world's second largest population of people infected by HIV? Yet my passion and work had only left me with more pain. I had lost my home, lost my country, and lived in despair, and now I found myself handcuffed and tossed *to* and *fro* by immigration officers.

In Nigeria, there was an underlying discrimination by health-care providers to MSM since the law that criminalized same-sex marriage and sentenced offenders to fourteen years of imprisonment was passed in 2014 by Pres. Goodluck Ebele Jonathan. He was from Bayelsa State, which was also from the Niger Delta region of Nigeria. Research had shown that there had been a drop in access to health-care services by MSM who fear being stigmatized.

A friend of mine said, "I hid myself very well for them not to call me names or something of that nature. Since I met that nurse who called me a ritualist and prostitute, I have not recovered from it up till now, you understand? So where am I now? I am just hiding so they cannot see any fault and call me names."

This discrimination had contributed to Nigeria ranking as second in the prevalence of HIV, and the incident rate was alarming. A recent study among gay men in Abuja found out that out of eight hundred gay men who started the study at baseline, 42 percent of them became HIV positive in thirteen months, yet the government did not see this as a problem. Most gay men I know were forced to get married and fulfill the wishes of their parents, their wives then giving birth and keeping their inheritance intact. Most of these men were not happy getting married against their own will and they still have sex with other men, get infected, and return to their wives. Then having sex with their spouse without protection led to the women also getting infected, with no proper diagnosis for maternal HIV and treatment available to prevent mother-to-child transmission.

The stigma perpetrated by religious institutions and the cultural backlash had found a home in the hearts of my people. My friend who was a victim of religious stigma and discrimination, like myself, lamented to God in prayers, always praying, "God, I do not want to deviate from Christian belief. I asked God. I did not create myself like this. You made me who I am. You said you knew me before I was born, before my mother conceived me. You know that am going to live this life. So if it is bad, why did you create me?"

He was always afraid he was offending God because of the teaching he heard from his pastor every sermon. He would say that gays were going to hell and would be destroyed by a wide lake of fire.

In the room at the detention center, my friend Jean was very helpful, but I could not stand the isolation and feelings I had of loss and grief. I was filled with hate, always thinking of hurting myself to stop the pain. I was in that mood when the officer asked us to line up to pick up the gift items that were distributed by a nonprofit group. The items in the folder I received were a pen, pencils, white A3 papers, envelopes, and stamps. In the package, there was also a letter, which I read, that was captioned "You are not alone." This meant a lot to me. Everybody was talking about this organization and how they provide support to detainees. I was intrigued by the explanation Jean gave me of how they have supported him through his nine-month stay in the detention.

I picked up the phone and called First Friends of New Jersey and New York, the organization that also sends volunteers to visit people who are detained, isolated, and have no family or friends. Isolation is a disease that can kill faster than cancer, damage your brain cells, and leave you hopeless. On the other end of the call was a lady with a beautiful voice. Her name was Sally, and she attended to me with care and referred me to another lady, Rosa, the coordinator of visitation. She introduced herself and told me to hold on, that someone would come to visit me. I was very happy at the way they treated me like a human.

One Saturday in late November, almost one month after I had first been put in the detention center, I applied for a job at the detention center. I was introduced to working in the kitchen by the Africans who advised me to keep my mind busy by participating in the daily routine. I would usually go to the kitchen by 10:30 a.m. and return for the 2:30 p.m. afternoon shift because for us, not much time would be wasted doing this work. Otherwise, we would sit in our rooms, praying for the next day to come. But working in the kitchen gave us the opportunity to eat extra food that would have been thrown away, to fill our bellies, and earn one dollar in our commissary account. It was a good deal, a toast to the good life and better than none.

That day, I got to work very early, but the kitchen officer asked me to report to the visitation desk because I had a visitor. I was accompanied to the visitation room by an officer, and I felt anxious and at the same time happy to hear I was being visited. An old lady walked up to me and called me by my name, Nong Richie. This was the very first time I felt like a human and for someone to call me just by my name since I had arrived and lost my identity to a bed number.

We sat, and she introduced herself. "Hi, my name is Lillian Zwyns, and I am here to visit you with my friend Cliff. We're members from a meditation group, and we usually come to visit."

"Thank you, Lillian. I am pleased to see you," I replied, and then we discussed life outside the detention wall. She told me it was not easy in America since she had also lived through different times where there was no telephone, when she had studied abroad in Germany, and how she always had written her mother loads of letters. I had not known we were going to be exchanging letters, but she gave me her address and told me I was free to write her anytime I wanted. I told her how I felt when she called my name, that since I came, they had been calling me by my bed number, Bed 26. But now I don't want that bed anymore because people who had previously slept on that bed had been deported.

When she left, her visit lasted with me for as long as time would permit, and I was feeling happy. My mood was light when I returned to my room, and I shared my experience of the visitation room with the other detainees.

During the same week, my best friend won his asylum. He was from Eritrea and occupying bed 8, so his bed would become empty. Before he left, he gave me a little narrative of how all the Africans who were previous occupants of bed 8 ended up winning their cases.

"What a lucky bed!" We both smiled. So I applied and changed my bed. The night my friend left, I lay on bed 8, thinking of how long it would take for my turn to leave the detention center. I had still not seen any place in the United States, except the beautiful lighting of New York City and a beautiful painting of New York City neatly placed in the visiting room of the detention center and old movies I had watched. I still have in my head a picture of the beauty of America and my dreams of living freely.

Lillian and I would begin this wonderful relationship of messaging each other with letters and sharing words of comfort, all of which kept me going at difficult times. My encounter with Lillian and her sharing her experiences with me were not short of magical.

The struggles of living in a detention center did not end by getting the lucky bed number 8 as I only began to understand that the United States had four weathers. Winter was fast approaching, and it would be my first winter. Although I was in a jail, freezing temperatures knew no boundaries or walls. I was watching the news and heard warnings of climate change and how it affected North America with violent storms and blizzard temperatures. I heard how President Trump had been elected and was sending out staggering tweets of how he would build the wall. All this increased the tension, fear, and anxiety for what would be the outcome of my Mexican brothers who complained in Spanish at the English commentaries and political commentators arguing what the deciding fate of immigrants will be, with the constant threats of deportation.

I knew nothing about the politics of America, but I was aware of the struggle to fulfill campaign promises during my days in college when I campaigned and contested for a position in the student union leadership and representation of my department and became the first nonindigenous president at Enugu State University. I was from Delta State; people of Enugu speak a different language, and they were among the Igbos who live in five southeastern states in Nigeria. They did not recognize me as a member of their ethnic group and did not see me as worthy of governing, even if we were from the same country. Division among ethnic groups played a major role in the political climate of Nigeria. I made my first attempt of becoming the department representative in 2011, and I lost the election by a slim margin. I had a rerun for the same position in 2012 with much resistance from my peers. My resilience and showmanship of good character and my strength in not giving up saw me through, and I became the first nonindigenous Igbo man to win a presidential student union election.

Being victorious affirms your positive mentality during times of trials, but when you are detained and bounded by large brick walls or when you have lost the meaning of your name to a bed number, it becomes difficult to think about the victories you have won. I was going to appear in court for the first time in my life and stand before a judge, and I was sitting in the waiting room, waiting for my turn to be called by the guard to stand before the judge.

I became alert when the guard was trying to call my surname, then I trembled as I walked with the guard toward the courtroom. I had heard of this immigration judge from other detainees who told me how strict she was and how she had a high denial rate for asylum. The immigration court was a quiet, well-furnished room, with just four people in it. The judge was seated in a higher place, the bench, a beautiful piece of furniture, and beside her was a lady on a typewriter. Another lady was standing beside me, the government lawyer, and then there was myself. I appeared before the judge who threw the first question at me, "Is your name Nong Richie?"

I replied, "Yes, my lord."

The quiet room was immediately overtaken by laughter. The judge asked, "Are you joking with me? I am not your Lord."

The government lawyer replied in my defense, "He is from Nigeria, and they are a British colony."

"Oh," the judge said, "I see the reason why. In America, we say 'Your Honor.'"

I replied, "Yes, Your Honor."

"Do you have a lawyer?"

"No," I replied. "I do not have a lawyer, Your Honor."

Then she gave me a list of pro bono lawyers. "Why did you come to court today?"

"I am seeking asylum." She gave me an asylum form and asked me to return to court with a lawyer the upcoming week.

I had met with some lawyers before who asked me to remain discreet as they prepared my case. I had been referred to this law firm by Immigration Equality. Immigration Equality is a nonprofit law firm in New York City that helps asylum seekers who identify as LGBT or HIV positive. They have a 99 percent win rate, and I was very confident when they told me a law firm under their network had been approved to represent me. The attorney from the other law firm had previously visited me and told me I had to open up to them and say the complete truth for them to give me an honest representation. They had introduced themselves. They were attorneys from Debevoise & Plimpton, and they looked very professional—all neatly dressed and the women were very pretty—and had a lot of compassion in how they looked at things. The pretty white lady told me she was going to be representing me, and her colleagues would support in making the draft. Altogether, five attorneys from the law firm would prepare me for my asylum application.

I started narrating my story to the attorneys, and when I was describing the attacks I suffered in Nigeria, the room was filled with tears and disbelief that humans from other parts of the world could be treated that way. She told me that she had never seen such dehumanizing treatment and would make sure I was granted justice. She also informed me of her preparation to apply for my parole so I wouldn't have to continue staying in the detention center. Then she and her colleagues took their bags and left.

Two days before my next court hearing, I was disturbed, thinking I would go to the court without a lawyer because I had not heard from the law firm. I got a mail that Friday from the law firm Debevoise & Plimpton. It came in a neatly packaged FedEx envelope with writing on top, saying Priority Mail and Overnight Delivery. Everyone admired the kind of package I had received, and when I opened this piece of mail, I found that my parole application had been submitted and the asylum form was filled out and ready for me to submit at my next court hearing. My attorney had also highlighted instructions of what to say in front of the judge.

That particular weekend could not come to an end sooner, as I was counting the hours to get to Sunday as quickly as possible. I spent that weekend watching my favorite shows and English soccer games, hoping my parole outcome would be positive, telling my fellow detainees that my stay would come to an end in less than seven days as soon as I received the result from Immigration Equality on the outcome of my parole. I very much believed I would be going out soon, and my attorneys were also confident of the draft they sent in. I had my haircut that weekend.

Monday finally arrived, and when call for breakfast was made, I quickly rushed into the shower, came out, and dressed in neat white socks and a T-shirt I had not worn before. I had little appetite to eat, and after breakfast, I was sitting at the door very close to the officer so I would not miss the call to be in court before count time. When I saw the officer with the names of detainees who would be attending court that morning, I stood up and waited for my bed number to be called out. I was among the three detainees from my dorm going to court that morning. It was time to show myself before the immigration judge again. When we got to the waiting area, I grew impatient, waiting for my name to be called. One detainee after the other was leaving the waiting room. Then the waiting area, which was filled to capacity, opened up, but it was not yet my turn. My confidence level dropped; the tension in the room dawned on me, along with the reality that the fate of people was being decided. Some of us would be deported that day by a judge's decision; others would be granted permission to stay. And lastly, a few would be given bond.

The toilet in the open room where people who were tense had urinated became really uncomfortable. As I was inhaling this offensive odor, it became a natural fragrance when my tension increased. The guy remaining with me in the room could feel my unrest. Finally, my name was called, and I walked slowly through the passageway, terrified because I had not come with a lawyer and the last judge had told me to return with an attorney. However, my lawyer had given me a document to give to the judge, so why was I now afraid?

I walked into the courtroom, and this time, there were about occupants in the room. Two elderly folks were sitting in the courtroom to support their visitor who happened to be the last man standing in the waiting area. They were there to stand for him in solidarity and support.

The judge was very friendly and asked me if I was among the gay men of Nigeria.

My response was yes, and I was smiling.

"You were asked to come with a lawyer. Where is your lawyer?"

I replied, "Your Honor, she gave me this document to give to you."

He collected it from me and read it. "Your application for asylum?"

"Yes, Your Honor," I replied.

"I will give you three months to prepare. Gather up the supporting documents, and come and defend yourself in March 2017."

"Thank you, Your Honor." And then I was escorted out of the courtroom.

I returned to my room, happy that I had ninety days to count down to my freedom. Sadly, my Nigerian roommate in the Gulf dorm would be leaving in two weeks. Still, it was almost Christmas, and I felt confident I would not spend my holiday with the detainees because of my confidence in my parole application.

I was warmly welcomed by the Nigerian guy in the Gulf dorm, who asked me how my court hearing had gone. I was trying to narrate the dilemma between me and the judge when one of the Tanzanians came with his friend. He had met them on the plane, and we called them the Zanzibar twins. They had flown on the same flight and were detained from the Newark Liberty International Airport just across the detention center.

I could read and write in English, which was a treasure in the detention center filled with immigrants from non-English-speaking countries. I had an advantage thanks to Nigeria having been a British colony. The Tanzanians asked me if I could help him reply to a letter that was sent to him by his First Friends visitor. I stopped my conversation and helped the men reply to their letters.

The visitor friend had taken some photos of their home and work area to give them a feel of the outside world. Furthermore, the letter said, "Do not lose hope because you will join me soon on the outside world . . . America is bigger than the four walls of a detention center."

When it snowed, we saw some glimpse of snow, which flooded the roof of the volleyball court; the volleyball court was a closed arena where we participated in outdoor games, as described by the facility. The court had pigeonholes found in the roof, which allowed natural elements to go through, but the Zanzibar twin, out of curiosity, wanting to have a feel of the snow, asked the officer if they could touch the snow on their way to the kitchen for night shift. When they returned from the kitchen, they asked me to narrate the feeling to their First Friends visitor in a letter. Freedom is a treasure, but only a few realize, and human wants are insatiable. Even with the most treasured freedom we seek, humans still remain in misery, wishing they had more.

A holiday was different in a detention center. You watch television and see people celebrate with their family while you remain locked up in a room far away from family and friends, living with people you never imagined you would have met from different parts of the world, all of us bounded by a single desire for freedom. My holiday was seasoned by a visit on the twenty-fourth of December 2016 by a friend nicknamed the Batman, whom I had met in Nigeria a few days before my arrival in the United States. He worked for the United States government, and when I met him in Abuja, the federal capital of Nigeria, he had extended me an invitation to his party. He usually holds a party on the twenty-first of December every year to celebrate the winter solstice. He had had the party and asked about me, but I was nowhere to be found. He told me I had been missed at the party because of my cheerful spirit, and this led to him searching for me. Finally, he was told by a Nigerian living in New York that I had been detained by immigration at the border, and he quickly remembered that I had discussed with him in Abuja about the hardship I faced based on my work as a human rights activist and the difficulty faced by MSM in accessing treatment. He was well equipped with the established facts, which was why he was nicknamed the Batman. He had worked with LGBTQ folks in Asia, in Africa, and in South America who experienced the same hardships faced by LGBTQ West Africans.

I was so glad to receive such a warm visit. He asked how I was doing, and I told him, "This is better than being dead in Nigeria." We had a long chat, which was cut off by the officer calling "Time up" since we were only allowed one hour of visiting per detainee. On Saturday, most especially, detainees' families come to visit, and the visitation room is filled to maximum capacity. The visitation room could only take about twelve detainees. The room had beautiful tables arranged and colorful paintings of New York City and the Statue of Liberty.

I was sad going back to my room, leaving my friend to return to the world and me to my room of forty-four isolated guys. Many detainees who had stayed in the US and overstayed their visa narrated how wonderful it was celebrating Christmas with family and friends in the United States, with the bright lighting of New York and the ball dropping in Times Square on the thirty-first. We knew our fate; we were going to spend our Christmas holding on to our fate, wishing to be granted freedom in the New Year.

When I was younger and still in Warri, it was on a Christmas Eve that I experienced my first interaction with the police. I was caught throwing fireworks, and the policemen detained me at the Warri divisional police station until my mom came with some military men who used their influence, and I was immediately released. Now I only wished my friend Batman had such influence to take me away from the arms of immigration.

CHAPTER FOUR

Setbacks

Sad news can be so disheartening to receive. In the month of December, the immigration officer came to my room to deliver a piece of mail on the decision of my parole request. When I got back to my dorm from the gym, the dorm guard told me that I had received a piece of mail from the immigration officer, and everyone who had been told of my parole request was excited and thought that I had received good news and would leave soon. When I opened the mail, to my disappointment, it was a denial letter, a news from the immigration officer that my parole was denied.

The 5:00 p.m. sun was down; night could not come to an end earlier. It was time to start counting each day and hoping it would come to an end. I wrote my First Friends contact, Lillian, of the court decision, and she was very comforting in telling me that this was not the end of the fight. She told me I should learn how to breathe and control my fear with practicing meditation, reading, and continuing my work in the kitchen to keep me busy.

My holidays would be more disastrous with this news, and I was trying to figure out if I was still dreaming, if all this was a reality. Then the winter started with me falling ill. I was shivering in my bed, and my fellow detainees called for medical attention, but for two hours, no one responded because it was a weekend. This wait led to an impatient riot by my dorm mates who asked to see the warden of the facility, emphasizing that someone was seriously sick in their dorm and that they didn't want to witness the death of a fellow detainee. The warden sent the supervisor to see me, and she saw I was running very high temperatures and then asked me to join her in the medical center. She kept me there for about another hour before a nurse came and checked me and gave me a pack of ibuprofen.

On the eve of Christmas, this illness had started, and on Christmas Day, I saw no significant improvement. On special holidays, detainees had the opportunity to eat chicken legs, but I was ill and had lost my appetite for just about anything. What a shame. I had severe nasal congestion, which started on Christmas Day. My favorite officer came to my bedside, and she felt pity for me for not being able to show my smile and uplift the spirit of my dorm mates who were mostly watching television all throughout the day. I was struggling in disbelief that I was spending my holiday in this place, and I could not sleep for all my thinking.

I was feeling much better before New Year's Eve. We had had a conversation about the ball dropping in Times Square, and most detainees had made plans to stay up late and watch the ball. I was a little depressed by this news and my health in the past week. Nothing interested me as it used to, and I fell asleep before 12:00 a.m. as planned. Only a few minutes into my sleep, I heard a roar, with the detainees jumping as if the gates of the detention center had been lifted and we were all asked to leave. I was still on my bed and not in the mood for silly games. When someone came close to my bed, tapping the brick wall, I rose to the scene, walked up to him, and was so filled with anger I was trying to unleash my venom on him. He was shocked by my reaction as he had never seen me in that state before.

He explained, "Hey, my guy, it's New Year. We're all celebrating."

I just replied, "I am not in the mood of celebrating." And then I returned to my bed. I was thinking of my reaction against a fellow detainee and remembered how my friend Lillian had told me that if I was feeling emotional, I should relax, breathe, and study my breath, then breathe in. *I know am breathing in and breathing out. I know I am breathing out.* I love Lillian, who taught me so much about patience and how to hold on and to believe there is light at the end of the tunnel.

The worst news came from my immigration lawyers and Batman—that some of my friends and colleagues in Nigeria had refused to write letters in support of my asylum proceeding. My feeling of helplessness worsened. I was saying to myself constantly, *If I was allowed access to the internet or free international phone calls, I would have written my friends myself.* The most hurtful news was that the executive director of the organization I worked for in Nigeria had refused to send a letter and had also asked my colleagues not to. This news hurt me badly because my executive director was a gay man too while my family and me were not in good communication because of my work and perceived sexual orientation. From the frying pan to the fire, news broke every now and then that left me thinking everything was bizarre.

Batman came to visit me in the New Year, and we chatted and tried to find a solution to the response from my executive director and colleagues in Nigeria. I told him the situation had left me helpless and that since the news came in, I had not been able to concentrate. But I was holding on to the practice my First Friends visitor had taught me. Batman offered to write me a letter of support for my asylum and also to stand as a witness in court on my final court day. This brought a lot of encouragement to a man who had almost lost hope.

I had now gotten a representative, so I called my lawyer to share this great news with her, but she gave me some difficult news to accept: her wedding was coming up on April 21 in Texas, and the immigration judge had extended my court hearing to April 18. Thus, she might not be able to represent me as she would be preparing for her wedding. My countdown had been extended six more weeks—six more weeks I had to continue staying at the detention center.

When I returned to my bed that day, I could not speak with anyone. I refused to eat dinner and was just quiet. My Nigerian roommate had won his case and left, my Eritrea friend had gone, and the two Ethiopian guys sharing space with me had also left. I was going to be here six more weeks, and how would I cope? I broke the news to Lillian, who always held her peace and mindfulness of everything. Again, she asked me to relax and think of the ocean, to let my mind be as clear as the deep blue ocean. Everything happens for a reason. She reminded me of my lawyers' statement that I had a strong case. My immigration attorneys also wrote me a letter to comfort me in this time of distress.

During my time in college, I had some heroic moments like winning the election and some horrible moments I never would wish any student to experience. One of these moments stuck in my memory. In 2011, after I lost my first student union election, I was tired of pretending and wanted to give myself a break. I was tired of using women as a defense and cover-up, of showing my colleagues that I possessed the characteristics of a worthy representative. The women friends also spoke their language, were in a different grade, and could convince more people than me alone. The society had been structured so that as a gay man, I had to think this way and be untrue to myself in order to gain acceptance by the people.

I really wanted to exhibit the true feelings I had been hiding, and this led to my search online for a male partner. I searched one particular dating site, and the response was quick. I found a guy who sounded interesting and had a good profile. I would receive a lovely text message that he wrote me in the morning and night and each and every day from our first meeting online. He told me how lovely I was and how special I was due to my vulnerability and lust over unnurtured feelings, how I was someone who had always been rejected by my classmates for being a member of a different ethnicity. He told me all I needed to hear because for someone to tell me I was worthy of living meant a lot to me at that point of my life, so I tapped into the idea of meeting him. After two weeks of chatting online, he invited me over to Enugu town because I had expressed my fear of bringing him to my school because of the suspicion it would give rise to. I decided to go visit this guy in Enugu, and although my school was in Enugu State, I was in school at the Agbani campus in the rural area and he was in the city of Enugu. I took the public transportation. Enugu city buses were painted in yellow with two black stripes on the side. I was excited to meet this man who really cared for me and had a beautiful name—Greg.

On arrival in Enugu town, I had some light snacks at the motor park and ordered a car rental service to take me to our agreed meeting place. Rule number 1 on gay dating in Nigeria was to not meet him in his place on the first date, but I did not know this as I was new to online dating and no one had provided me counsel. He had also made me feel comfortable by telling me he would not meet me in his own place but would be in front of the army barracks in Enugu. This is the Eighty-Second Division Army barracks, a prestigious Nigerian military base dating to the support it provided in conquering the Biafra territory during the Nigerian Civil War. The plan had been carefully made by Greg, for meeting there was part of his plot. When I drove closer to the barracks, I was afraid, but I was unaware of the schemes of what would be my attackers. I saw a cluster of men standing by the overhead bridge. The bridge was usually busy, so I was wondering, *What is my business with it?*

Greg was standing on the roadside, and once I came out of the car, he walked me into the school building opposite the barracks. He was having a conversation with me, so I thought he was going to discuss with me when next to meet, but less than two minutes into the conversation, two other guys walked behind me and asked me not to say a word but just to walk straight up into the classroom. A guy was waving in front of me in the specific classroom they were taking me to, then they took me to the old, empty space and threw me into one destroyed and no-longer-functioning classroom. A man spoke in pidgin English, "Hey, you see say we don screen munch all our chats, ba? And if you don't cooperate, we go hand you over to the soldiers and them go do you well. Well, you understand?" His speech meant, "Young man, we have saved our chats, and if you don't cooperate with us, we're going to hand you over to the military men who will beat you up and arrest you."

So I cooperated and handed over my phone to them first. They held me hostage there and took my ATM cards. Greg asked one of his boys to run to the nearest ATM machine and withdraw my entire balance. Before their colleague had returned, Greg searched me and took all the money I had in my wallet and then spitted on my face and said, "Faggot."

The distance from Enugu town to my campus was too far to walk, so I stood on the roadside, shamelessly asking for people on the street if they could help me with some cash to pay for transport back to school. I still had my school identity card on me.

This life I was living was a mess according to my dad, who had commented that nothing good could come from me.

I started believing the narrative that nobody wanted me. I was going from one attack to another with ongoing persecution in my country, and my beloved community was not supporting me at this point. Furthermore, most people wanted me dead in Nigeria, and the United States Immigration might not grant me protection because I did not have the needed supporting documents. And words were not good enough to convince a judge who had presided over hundreds of immigration cases. I was terrified as to what would be my fate.

All hope seemed lost. I was afraid to use the phone because my lawyer told me of the deadline to file the supporting documents was fast approaching. Now I was a little grateful the judge had given an extension. "It is a blessing" were Lillian's words. Anxious of the outcome, I felt restless and confused, most of the time quiet as if my mouth was taped shut, lying in my bed.

After my kitchen work on Easter weekend, I received another mail package from my immigration attorney. I quickly opened it, wishing it was not bad news, that they had dropped my case because of lack of evidence or my attorney would not be able to represent me because of her wedding. It was a very heavy large file that had come in the mail in a FedEx package with pieces of papers put together in a textbook-style binding. I opened the letter and read the first pages. It was my declaration for asylum followed by pages of evidence collected by my attorney and her team. She and Batman had contacted my friends on my behalf. The Nigerian guy in New York City who had told Batman I was being detained by immigration also submitted a letter to support my case. One of the pieces of evidence written on it was the call for my execution by the community in Abuja where I lived. Seeing this latter piece, I became more afraid of what would be the outcome of my life if the judge denied my application.

Abuja is the capital city of Nigeria, located in the center of the country within the Federal Capital Territory (FCT). It was a planned city and was built mainly in the 1980s, replacing the country's most populous city of Lagos as the capital on December 12, 1991. Abuja's geography is defined by Aso Rock, a 400 m (1,300 ft.) monolith left by water erosion. The presidential complex, National Assembly, Supreme Court, and much of the city extend to the south of the rock. Zuma Rock, a 792 m (2,598 ft.) monolith, lies just north of the city on the road to Kaduna State. Abuja, which used to be the safe haven for people, had now lost the sanctuary coverage since the passage of the Same Sex Marriage Prohibition Act in 2014. This law had led to a lot of violent mob attacks and jungle justice for people with this perceived sexual orientation. Jungle justice or mob justice is a form of public extrajudicial killings in Sub-Saharan Africa, most notably in Nigeria and Cameroon, where an alleged criminal is humiliated, beaten, or summarily executed by a crowd or vigilantes.

This was the persecution I would have to face, along with humiliation in a public space, if I was caught by the community members in Abuja before I traveled to the United States. And Batman, who understood this terrain and would have helped me explain it to the judge, sent me a letter that he would have to be traveling for a meeting and would not be able to make the final court hearing.

Letter of Lamentation to My Father

Daddy, you know I had the zeal and willingness to put pen to paper. That's why you tell me to inform you five weeks before the last date of chasing students who have not paid fees for the school year. I am grateful for your contribution to my birth by donating your sperm, but other than that, you have never been there for me. I know you tried your best. Unlike others who do not have the money to pay for their children's school fees, you had the money, but you preferred to gamble with your hard-earned cash rather than to buy me pencils and erasers to sharpen my knowledge.

You made my sisters and elder brother laughing stocks in the community, to such extent that it felt like my siblings were not serious with life. If you had stayed with my mother and cared for your children, you would have not suffered in the hands of polygamy. As you had explained to me as a child that experience is the best teacher, now I am replying to you as an adult that education is the best legacy. You can testify with your experience of polygamy; I can testify to the importance of education. I remember vividly the last time I asked you for school fees, and you replied to me and my sisters that good students reminded their fathers of their fees every day continuously for two weeks if they were really serious. Now I am replying to you with my own voice: good fathers care about their children and inquire of their fees before the start of the school year so they can save and plan toward paying.

Thank you for bringing me to this world, but no thanks for not showing up in any PTA meetings, sports games, and extracurricular activities. I felt like an orphan right from my childhood and now in my adulthood. I am replying to you in my own voice: no thanks for the role you played as an absent figure all along.

Daddy, you are still alive, but your absence resonates.

CHAPTER FIVE

Freedom in Disguise

April showers brought May flowers. It was windy outside, clouds had become thicker, and the Creator had marked that day in April for the gates to be lifted. I walked outside of the courtroom, thankful for the decision I got.

"We all get swept away by the big and small things of life from time to time, but it always brings a smile to my face (and a couple of tears of joy to my eyes) when I think about how happy we all were when the judge finally approved," Emily said. There had been nights and days of hard work, countless reviews, and excellent preparation by the team of five attorneys, spearheaded by the beautiful white lady.

I met with my attorneys after the court hearing, and Batman was also there. He was truly a super friend. He was supposed to be in South Africa for a meeting, but his flight was canceled as he told me, and he had made it to the court. He was there when the judge granted a decision in my favor, and now it was time for him to go back to his duties. He flew to South Africa that same day, so for me, now all hope was lost for housing. I had thought I was going to stay in his place for some time, but now he was traveling, so I had good and bad feelings at the same time, both victory and a vacuum.

By 6:00 p.m., plates and forks were clinking. The men of the Gulf dorm were somber, especially the Tanzanian twins, who always sat by my bed when I told stories of how I dreamed we were all going to be free one day and shared words of hope when we were all in despair.

I remember one of the guys walking up to me, saying, "Nong, I will really miss you. You are very cheerful when you are in good spirits." The

Spanish- and French-speaking folks were really sad that one of their best letter writer was going. I had grown accustomed to the life in detention, and now I felt scared to even face the brave new world out there. I was in the middle of figuring out what life would be like outside detention.

I heard voices sounding like a tsunami, roaring like a hurricane's wild wind, moving like a cyclone. And they disrupted my fear, anxiety, and panic.

"Hey, Bed 8, it's time to go pack up." At this point, I was lying on my bed trying to catch some sleep, but the excitement of my soon leaving the walls of the detention kept me awake. Many of my friends were writing on pieces of paper their alien registration number and commissary account number and asking me to write them letters and send some cash when I started working out there. I was happy to rise from my bed, cheered by the entire dorm, and to walk toward the door with a bag I had made from my bedsheet hanging over my shoulder like a slave that had been emancipated by his owner.

Now was the time to start a new life; the long wait had yielded the required result. I got to the waiting room, the officers gave me my belongings, and the gate was finally lifted. It was about 10:00 p.m. in the night, and it was raining. The streetlights were very bright, illuminating my way to freedom. I hadn't known where I am, surrounded by warehouses and no means of transportation, but freedom tasted good. When the slaves were freed from their masters, they had no place to go because servitude was the only life they had known, so they stayed back in the plantation. Although I knew no place, going back to the detention center was not an option for me, so I walked out into the rain. I could feel the cleansing power of the showers. It was spring, and that was the birth of my new life, my journey to find a new home.

Never in my life had I felt relieved like I felt that day. A few months ago, I had been the man running and hiding from people who refused to accept me for who I am, and now I was walking free. I had not enjoyed a good meal in months, and I was very glad the day my dorm was given two boxes of pizza because we won the neatness challenge. A slice of pizza that cost ninety-nine cents was like a prized jewel in the hands of detainees. Freedom comes with a price, and I had paid my price with countless days in isolation, defending who I am and how I had lived my life in the past decade. Nobody, given such a priceless opportunity, would want to throw it into a shark-infested water.

The question from the beginning was this: why do people who seek freedom still have to go through such hardship to get freedom? There is a global refugee crisis of over sixty-five million displaced people, and some percentage can be attributed to the harsh laws against LGBTs in eighty-plus countries. It is a well-established fact that a country has lost some of its brightest talents as thousands flee to countries with favorable laws. Living in denial does not erase the fact that these laws affect the economic growth of countries that throw away their talents—those of entrepreneurs, writers, artists, athletes, and academics.

Now my fear had become a reality. Where would I go? How would I have a roof over my head when the temperatures were not friendly? How would I have a warm meal for my stomach when I had less than forty-two dollars in my pocket?

Asylees, refugees, and immigrants are being traumatized by this process, and some people who feel entitled are not receptive to humans who have gone through so much in order to step through the door into America. For a man who has gone through this trauma, what relationship does he have with the economy of a country he just arrived in when his primary goal is simply survival? When people are in survival mode, luxury is less likely an option. Despite this struggle by immigrants, refugees, and asylees, some Americans still complain that immigrants are taking their jobs.

Coming as I did from the thick rain forest of Southern Nigeria where I grew up, I had never seen structures as magnificent as what I saw that night. Neatly tired roads filled me with awe that my empty stomach lost its appetite for food.

Then an angel arrived. She drove in an SUV, stopped, and called my name.

"Are you Nong?"

Earlier in the day, I had spoken to First Friends of New Jersey and New York, and they had promised to send me a volunteer to pick me up. Here was the volunteer, and she told me she would take me to a shelter in Newark, New Jersey, to the YMCA.

That night, sleep did not come, and I stayed awake, thinking of options I had had before requesting asylum at the border. Many people in the detention center told me I had made a wrong decision by asking for asylum at the border, that I should have crossed and looked for a place to stay after a while before applying for asylum. I never knew I would go through such a dehumanizing treatment. Instead of upholding my courage for standing for what was right, I was insulted, I was made to enjoy broad daylight slavery by working for a dollar at the detention center, guarded by untrained staff who regarded humans as less than their worth and shamed their identity as immigrants from countries that were unstable, and I was placed in isolation with no psychologist to help talk you through the trauma you faced in your home country.

The condition countries like Nigeria are in can be largely attributed to the colonization by developed countries who milked away our natural resources, used my forefathers' man power to build wealth and acquire our labor force through human trafficking. Yes, I had an option of not asking for asylum at the border, but what difference does it make if either way I could not survive the hardship of being undocumented and not being able to work for up to two years? How would I be able to feed myself and have a roof over my head? My friend who moved to the United States a year before me had not yet gotten documents to work, and his asylum process took him eleven months just to file to immigration. He was as good as an internally displaced person in the United States, moving from one friend's house to another, suffering sexual abuse from hosts, and constantly terrified by the change in government and immigration policies.

We must surely put an end to the persecution of LGBT persons, which leads to immigration, for we do not know who would be victims tomorrow, seeking protection in another country and being treated like criminals, keeping them in private prisons and making profit from them. This is not the life I would wish for anyone, not even my enemy.

There is no place like home, but globally, people have lost their homes because of this antigay law. In more than eighty countries, laws still exist that persecute people who are identified as a member of the LGBTQ community in Nigeria—my home country—for a case study. This was contributing to the global crisis of immigration that had left an estimate of sixty-five million people displaced from their homes, with it taking an average of seventeen years to be resettled in a new country. For me, the fact that is difficult to digest is, there are gays everywhere, and you cannot stop the existence of humans. Gays are humans, and they should be granted freedom of association as people are granted the freedom of speech and of religious choice.

I cannot overemphasize the dangers of antigay laws and the lack of human rights protection by the government in these eighty-plus countries. When I made the decision to leave home, it was not my choice. Many people like me had made such a decision, and I thought they were looking for a better life. Their search had led them to immigrate. But my thoughts were wrong. It was hostility that led to their immigration, the inefficiency of their government to protect them, and the hostility suffered by these many refugees and asylees who came to the United States from a country in the throes of upheaval.

Decisions like this are breathtaking, definitely life changing. It definitely cost me my entire life's struggles—with my primary education, college degree, master's degree, culture, language, and lifestyle all gone within a wink of an eye. It was bravery—not bravery to let go of all I had struggled for but bravery to have saved my life. What is most surprising is how friends and families have decided to easily let go of you and wish you death because of misinformation, prejudice, and comfortability with the known. They are afraid of the unknown and are threatened by change. Generation to generation, this teaching has been passed on, and no one wants to question what they have been brought up to understand as normal. The thought of doing it alone is frightening, and I can testify to those circumstances. I lost faith in myself and my abilities because everything they did was constantly criticize me. If my friends could have been more loving and if they tried to hear my inner voice, that was all I could ask for. Was it too much for some to just sit and listen? We were blinded by a single story of our generation, and we successfully ran into the trap of smart and crafty men who designed the system to give meaning to their ideologies and to hide the power of their knowledge in books. This was the weak point for a typical Nigerian—to think he had learned everything from what he had read in books.

This single story damaged me as a child and made me a f——prejudiced individual. Since my childhood, I always had loved soccer games, and I loved watching my favorite team, Arsenal of London, which happened to be the soccer team of my elder brother. This made me develop an interest in the game, and I wanted to be a soccer player. I would stand in the stadium and watch guys playing soccer, and I decided to join a soccer team in my street in Warri called Bobby Boys. The guys in this area were crazy about this game, and they placed bets on sides to win and even scouted for young boys to put them into professional soccer teams in Europe and South America. My intention was to train and be a better soccer player, but I was met with the same judgment I would grow up to suffer. I was a typical laughing stock. Boys and girls would mock me and say that I played the game like a woman. This shaming led me to abandon my passion and my dream to be a professional soccer player, and instead, it led me to stay at home and watch my favorite team in England.

My father would constantly criticize girls who wore pants as he believed that anyone who was brought up by a decent father and in a morally competent home should not expose her body parts. My elder sister who was only sixteen years old became pregnant although she never wore pants, always attended church with my parents, and was always a good girl who did what my parents wanted. How come she became pregnant? It happened; prejudice had left them clueless. The hunter had caught an elephant and did not know where to start eating from it. Similarly, I was brought up to believe that people with tattoos were gang leaders and criminals and that a girl who wore pants was a prostitute, and these were the basic Christian values of a Nigerian. The mind is so shallow when it constantly feeds on the same view.

What makes a left-handed person less human than a right-handed person just because right-handed persons are the majority in our society? After a while, my sister was accepted by my family, and my dad made a statement that it was only a mistake and misinformation to a teenager that had led her to becoming pregnant. Now I think to myself, *Why would my family not accept me too? Is it just because they think gay men are involved in witchcraft so they do not deserve to live by the philosophy of a traditional African man?* Families have lost ties with their children; many have led their children into drug addiction and thoughts of committing suicide because of tradition that was designed by humans like myself. I wanted to commit suicide because I felt it was my only escape from the constant humiliation I faced.

I would have considered other methods of immigration, even if I had been left alone to use the unconventional route of taking a ship across the ocean. Nothing would have stopped me because I was desperate to be free, and I believed that just across the ocean, people could live, breathe, practice the religion of their choice, and still be who they are.

I had come late to my church this particular Sunday, and the auditorium was filled to capacity, so I was standing in the overflow when this smart, neat, handsome-looking guy walked through the middle gate of the cathedral. He was being guarded and escorted by security out of the building. *What is the issue?* I asked myself, but there was no one to talk to in a sanctuary, and all my family members were sitting at the front row, listening to the sermon. To my amusement, I prejudged the man to be an important person, a VIP, because as a norm, rich people and politicians were always followed by escorts in Nigeria. However, this guy had been walked out of the church for wearing earrings, and the minsters said that he was going to corrupt younger ones in the church. Men, by no means, should wear earring or rings, except the rebellious ones. I cannot judge the society; I am only pointing out to the society what they consider to be good. That guy was accepted back to the congregation when he took off his earring, but how could I take away my sexuality?

The struggle of my childhood was categorized by this narrative of feeling inadequate and trying to belong to the society. Young people drive me crazy when they try to make you realize that you are not part of the community because of your inability to show them the strength you possess. The slogan of this struggle is in the term "Warri boy," and the meaning of this term has become a cliché. When you want to show someone you are stronger than him or her, you use the word categorically in an aggressive manner: "You know say I be Warri boy shey," meaning "Warri boys are tough. Don't mess with me." Everyone who identifies with this cliché only brags about their lack of knowledge most of the time. This narrative had made me struggle more to impress people that were from the town or to feel accepted among the crowd. The society I grew up in had classified me into a box, a definite position they felt I should stand in and represent.

My mother always called me when I was living in the city of Abuja and explained for hours on the phone how she dreamed of my wedding and how the woman would look like. This expectation set before me was basically due to the pressure she was receiving from her friends and her wanting me to meet the standards set by her friends. We all have different ambitions, dreams of how we want our life to be. How many of us live up to that dream? Only a few do, based on pressures from the society to fall into the category they assigned.

When I ran away from my family in Warri to live in Abuja, this decision was based on the demands I faced every day from my family, who were trying to arrange a girl for me to marry. My mother contacted the vice president of her women's social club for a private meeting, and they had discussed how to bring a daughter to me and introduce her in a way that would lead to our starting a relationship because I would be so intrigued by her reactions. That fateful Saturday evening, my mother's friend named Morogun, who came from a very wealthy family in Warri and who was well respected for the expanse of land they acquired after the war, was coming to the house. Their family name rang a bell on the lips of friends and family, for it was every man's dream in Warri to marry into such a family. My mother was fortunate to have met her through their women's social club, and she had told her of her son. She wanted to meet me because she had heard of my achievement as the first college graduate of my family, for it was very rare for a family in the down side of Warri to have a child with a college degree. As I have mentioned earlier, Warri boys were more concerned about their physical strength than their brainpower.

I was in my room, and my mom called me to the living room where I met Mrs. Morogun and her daughter Esther. My goodness, Lord. Esther was a pretty young lady with a bachelor's degree in pharmacy from Delta State University. I greeted her and her mother and was walking over to take my seat on the floor of the living room when my mom started the conversation.

"Nong, you know Mrs. Morogun?"

I replied, "Yes, Mommy. They have all the houses on Morogun estate, am I right?"

"Yes," my mom replied. "Mrs. Morogun brought her daughter to see you. Is that not special?"

My head read the definition of what they were doing. My mom had arranged for me to marry a girl who was educated and was from a wealthy family, and the young lady was very responsive because her mom had decided for her to meet a college graduate and not a Warri boy.

My mom was narrating my biography to her. "Nong stayed with his aunt in another city, left Warri when he was young after the crisis, and got a college education from Enugu, eastern Nigeria."

She looked at me, and she was smiling. Mrs. Morogun was very proud of this stat, and my intention was also good. I didn't want to hurt her. I had feelings for women, but I was not prepared to get married. Should I not be allowed to make a choice for myself like my elder brother did? My elder brother had been able to successfully ask for the hand of three women in marriage before I got my college degree, in a typical display of "like father, like son."

The evening came to an end with me not having an opportunity to say a word. My mom collected her number and gave Esther my number, but that was the last day she would ever see me as I prepared to escape the next lady my mother might prepare to introduce me to. On the other hand, my eldest brother had been able to make himself the all-important inheritance to the kingdom. He had been able to secure his badge as the first son and is a proud father of two sons by the first two wives and a girl from the current wife. My mom wanted me to emulate his footsteps and have a child, which I do not object to, but I only wanted to make the choice at my own time.

In my family, my elder brother and two elder sisters all had a child out of wedlock. I was the only one who had fathered no child out of wedlock, but I was also the one they considered the least human. "How can a boy not have a child at your age?" they ask. In Warri, teenage pregnancy was something youths brag about, but I had promised myself to have a child only when I have enough to take care of one. Despite that, the pressures had become persistent, and the only way I could escape was to relocate to a different city far away from home.

My life had been a constant struggle, and I didn't want this constant struggle to be the pattern for the upcoming generation. The lives we have lost to homophobia are uncountable; families that have been destroyed by negativity are greater than the ones that accepted and loved their children abundantly. And the search for a new home was not an easy experience. The marginalization of immigrants by natives and the xenophobic attacks were not worth it. Instead, we need peace and love now more than ever before to heal the broken hearts and mend broken homes.

Letter from Julius in Port Harcourt, Nigeria

Dear Nong,

When I saw your video on YouTube, protesting in front of the Nigerian consulate, I smiled and remained proud of you. Even if the people of Nigeria are against us, I still believe in you. You fought so strongly and courageously when you were here. In your absence, we still feel your strength. When the world was against you, you still believed in yourself. You were such a good friend who stood by me and against those who are strongly homophobic in our society.

Nong, you suffered in the hands of blackmailers and fraudsters because of your true identity. You fought for me when I was denied medical rights and attention. You never let yourself down by telling the world how you felt being a free gay man.

My friend, the fight would have been stronger if I still have you by my side to help those who are jailed, to promote the message of love, and to provide support to those who are hiding in their shelves. Those who couldn't speak—you gave them the voice they desired. Those who needed someone to talk to—you gave them a listening ear. Those who needed good medical care—you helped them secure one.

It has always been your passion to speak, to fight for the rights of those whose rights have been denied, and to make the gay community a strong place where one is entitled to freedom. My dear friend, I really miss you, but even as you are no longer here to fight with me, I will always help those who struggle. I will keep your flag of pride up. I will make the world know that you existed. I will let the world know about your fight for your rights and the rights of all gays in your region.

I only wish and cry all the time when someone needs someone to speak up. People of your kind are rare to find, and it is my hope that people would rise up and fight to make our flag of pride be counted.

In your words, "I may be rejected today, but it does not mean I will stop fighting for my rights and the rights of all LGTBQ in my locality. The world must hear my voice and must end homophobia in my time." Your voice was not heard fully, but your dream must be known, and your fight must be won. My friend, keep fighting the good fight of faith.

CHAPTER SIX

The Agony of Being Gay in Nigeria

STORY OF MY FRIEND WISDOM IN WARRI

I have been struggling to live the life I always dreamed of, the life of freedom from discrimination and stigmatization for being effeminate, for it is really sad not to be able to do something you love.

On my ninth birthday, still in primary school, I had my first homosexual experience with an older guy, and this guy, whom I had my first sexual experience with, happened to be the betrayer. Now I wish I could have killed him when he did it to me the first time. If I were a sorcerer, I would have taken away his life by now. I had been carrying this burden of telling the truth about myself since I was nine years old. Life for me had not been easy as a silent gay man. I was sitting on the fence between the love I have for men and the backlash from the society, but still, I felt stronger connections toward men.

I do not know how to control my affections within my inner self, and I lost self-control of myself. I became a slave in my midlife crisis—slave to sex. I felt like nobody wanted me. My family did not understand me. I was rejected by society because of my effeminate looks, so I decided to become a sex trader. Prostitution became my practice, having sex with men who were masculine and financially independent. They told me my body was good and that I looked like a woman. For me, it was a win-win since I got help and my financial needs were met. I became the whore that society had labeled me.

I met with men in unusual places because they didn't want their wives to know they were having sex with a man. I was very happy when one of the men called me his first *iya* wife. I had sex with them in their offices or hotel rooms, and sometimes they'd sneak me into their matrimonial homes when their wives traveled. Even the fear of being caught made it more fun. With all the sex I had with these men, I still returned home and masturbated almost every night. This continued throughout my teenage life.

In 2015, my mom got to know about my sexuality, and I bluntly denied with all the tactics I had learned from my customers. I became a chief liar. My mom believed me and only wanted to clear her mind of the thought of me being a gay man. She decided to take me to her prayer meetings for the pastor to cleanse me of being gay; she also took me to different prayerhouses. Nothing changed within me, but I pretended to her that I felt something moving in my body. For me to convince her that I had changed, I stopped going out and satisfied myself with adult films. This could not satisfy me unlike the touch of a man, but I didn't want her to suffer from heartache because of the struggle she was going through herself. I would have considered having a steady relationship with one person, but I had suffered too many disappointments in my past. And the expectation of almost every gay Nigerian demands you look a certain way so they can walk with you on the street.

I hated myself and fell into depression. No one was there for me to speak to; no one understood me at this crucial point of my life. I had three lesbian friends whom I confided in for help—since lesbians do not suffer as much hatred as effeminate gay men like myself—and a gay friend of mine in Lagos who showed so much concern. He asked me to come over to Lagos and linked me up with a psychologist who also was a counselor for help. I was afraid of myself, and I needed help. I was afraid every single day. If people in my school get to know about me, the cult members would kill me.

I had seen the guy whom I had my first sexual experience with; he was now a converted Christian, feeding my mom with information and revelations he got of me being gay. I wish I could pretend like one of the hundreds of gays and lesbians who marry one another and pretend they are straight saints, but for me, it would double or triple my burden. Words really could not express how I felt about this. It broke my heart. If you continuously compete with others, you become bitter, but if you continuously compete with yourself, you become better. I am stronger than my past; the future is for all. I only wish parents would understand their children more and not contribute to society's demands and standards. It is my honest hope that many young Nigerians would have the opportunity to live a life free of stigma and discrimination like I did.

PERSONAL ACCOUNT FROM ZUBBY,
ASYLEE IN SAN FRANCISCO

I woke up that morning, as always, with no idea that an event was going to change my life forever. It was on the twenty-eighth of November 2008 in Jos, capital of Plateau State in North Central Nigeria. I was on my way to write a paper in school as we had ongoing exams in my university. I had noticed the city looked empty; I had also heard gunshots. I called my boyfriend, Charles, to make sure he was safe at the hostel. After that, our bus was pulled over, and everyone was asked to exit. The guys who pulled the bus over were not policemen. They were members of a local militia. They asked everyone on the bus, one after the other, if we were Muslim or Christian. I realized only those who were Muslims were allowed back on the bus. When it came to me, as soon as they asked me the same question, they asked everyone before me, people inside the bus shouted in Hausa language, "He is not Muslim. *Dandaudu Ni.*" It means "He is gay" in English. "He told a man on the phone, 'I love you,'" they chorused. It immediately occurred to me my phone speakers must have been too loud. I was hit with a plank on the back of my head, objects you would not imagine had been used on a wild animal. I was locked up for days, awaiting death, until I was aided to escape by one of them, who turns out he was secretly gay too. I still have nightmares from that experience till this day. This was before Same Sex Marriage Prohibition Act (SSMPA) passed in 2014. Post-2014, the risk of being perceived as gay was a scary thought for many people like me. I had many other experiences in the hands of the police, homophobic citizens, friends, and even family. It got to a point in my life when all I prayed about at night was to sleep and never wake up, and then when that never happened, I would consider for months ways to silently end my life. When I couldn't go through with that, I would fall into depression, cut everyone out, and just focus on work with a smile on my face while I was dying on the inside.

I came to the United States for a wedding reception and traveled around to see old friends and family. I mean, I have traveled before and even lived outside Nigeria for a while, but this time, I opened my mind to learn something new on this visit. Everywhere I visited, I began to see a difference with the way people treated the knowledge of my sexuality. I had friends who have died simply because they were gay. Vincent was beaten to death in his university. Emmanuel died of AIDS because he couldn't get the care he needed. Lawal was locked up in prison for months because the police found gay porn on his computer. Here, I was in a gay bar in broad daylight thousands of miles away from home, and that was when I realized that staying here in the United States was the best decision for me. Prior to that day at the gay bar, I had fought with the idea of leaving everything I had back home in Nigeria—my friends, my job, my family, and everything I knew and understood—and start a new life all over again. The thoughts of it scared me, but then I realized that my family and friends were not going through the same psychological issues I faced daily, and I think they are happy with their lives. I may have a good job and my life appeared okay, but the truth was that I wasn't happy. There were a lot of issues I was facing personally daily all because I was gay. The safety of my life was my everyday worry. All I had ever wanted in my life was to go to bed at night without guilt in my heart, without shame, without fear for my own safety. And finally, all I had ever wanted was to find happiness somewhere, somehow, someday. I left everything behind for two reasons—my safety and my happiness. Although life in the US was not as pleasant and perfect as how many people, especially in Africa, perceived it to be, but for a gay man like myself, the US felt more like home to me than Nigeria. In the short time that I had been here in the US, I learned so much, and now I know that I can achieve whatever goals I set for myself and live the life I have always dreamed about without fear or guilt or shame. The LGBT community in Nigeria only existed in the shadows, behind closed doors, and in small social groups. To my own knowledge, the LGBT youth in Nigeria was the most entrepreneurial and intelligent people I know—from makeup artists to fashion designers, doctors, and lawyers. Unfortunately, the Nigerian environment had made it impossible for many of us to flourish and succeed since members of the community lived in constant fear for their lives and safety.

The SSMPA made it terrible for LGBT people to focus on a career and life in Nigeria. It made a lot of us start considering life in another country where our lives can have meaning and where we can find safety. You know, sometimes I wish things were different back home. I wish there were no laws criminalizing who I am as a person. I wish I was home in Nigeria with my family and friends and eating all the food I grew up knowing. That, though, was not the case. I had come to realize that, indeed, immigration sometimes is not a choice but is necessary in others to save people from fear and hate. Also, I realized that home is where you are free to live the way that you choose. I am happy to be able to live here in America—a country that values freedom.

MY FRIEND'S ENCOUNTER WITH A
RECEPTIONIST AT A PHARMACY

A friend narrated to me his ordeal at the hands of a too-inquisitive drugstore attendant today.

He had gone to the said drugstore to get a condom and a lube. The place was bustling with impatient customers, each dishing orders around as though they were in some fancy five-star restaurant. He said he had respected himself and had taken solace in reading and refreshing his timeline and then repeating the entire process again to while away time and keep his mind away from the disarray in the store. When the number of customers had reduced to just one or two persons breezing in to check out something or throw in a gossip, he went to one of the attendants—a bespectacled young girl probably in her midtwenties—and placed his order. The girl ambled to a shelf and picked out two packs of condoms and a lube (both Durex) and walked back to the counter where she packaged it, registered it on their database, and asked him to go pay to the cashier and return for his item.

That was where the mgbese comes in.

As my friend went back to pick his goods, the auntie from the general commissioner of inquiry commission dropped the time bomb. "Excuse me, sir, don't be offended, but what are you using a lube for?" she asked, her face expressionless.

My friend was dumbfounded, shocked to the marrow. He took it as a fleeting jocular question, something not to lay so much credence on. "I am using it for sex," he answered, trying so hard to suppress the flush of embarrassment that was gradually sprawling across his face.

He thought the *Who Wants to Be a Millionaire* had ended, then suddenly, in the faintest voice he had ever heard in a human before, the weird geek added, "If you are gay, you better repent. That lifestyle is against the Word of God and the law of man. Several men have come in here these past weeks purchasing condoms and lubes. I know only homosexuals use lubes. God has naturally lubricated a woman for sex. Change your way, sir."

I couldn't help but laugh as my friend narrated this to me. I laughed at both the sheer audacity and the unprofessionalism of the "illiterate" attendant and the flagrant encroachment into the privacy of the customer.

Lamentation of a Friend in Nigeria

Dear Daddy—well, scratch that—just Daddy,

I know you had dreams for me, but what about my own dreams? You always thought it was me who would become a priest. You constantly tried to shut down my musical career, yet music was my go-to, my peace, my solace as I tried to embrace and understand that I was a different kind of man.

Mom was supportive. She knew I preferred dolls over cars when it came to toys. That was the reason we had so many conversations you and I could never have. She made an effort to know me deeply.

I am still a man, though—a man who is in love with another man. The laws and culture in Nigeria made it hard for me already. Why should I suffer the same prejudice and discrimination from my own father? I know you love me, but changing me won't be the best for me. If you could just accept me for who I am, we would be happier.

Love me for me as I love you for you.

Regards,

Dee

Lamentation of Jessy Dray, an Asylee

My name is Jessie Dray. I'm from a country where being human is treated like a mistake, where our rights are not recognized; to be precise it is a place of hate and fear. While I was growing up, I thought of myself as less of a human because of my personality being effeminate and because of my passion for music. I was living the life of someone. I refused to believe that I could exist because of so much hatred I built up for myself and because of the rejection from my parents. The community does not accept someone who is effeminate, and the country does not accept gays. My life was in shambles.

My life was a bunch of darkness when I was in Nigeria. I couldn't see through the eyes of my inner soul, longing to live freely and succeed in music. I was bitter, faced with shame whenever I move past people who cannot stop talking about me walking like a woman. I lived with discrimination from the nurse who called me an ass licker, with hate in my heart, and with war against myself, battling to behave in a way to gain the slightest support. I had been called a demon by my pastor and a faggot by my neighbor. People call me a sissy, and with so many harassments, I could not continue to live this life and I felt the best thing to do was to kill myself. I knew for sure people were born this way. I thought it wasn't my fault, but the community made me believe it was mine. This was not the life I planned or desired to live. It was unfortunate that I was born this way and had been treated less of a human. I was in the shadow of death, and everyone had the right to beat me or spit on me. I considered myself to be a curse sent from hell. I used to see myself just the way they saw me. I was barren to the reality of human rights. Nigeria was a living hell to me and to other males who were effeminate. Accepting myself to be who I am was not real, and just to live and be who you are were almost impossible. My soul hurt, and my heart melted. It burned my eyes and made my eyes bloody when it was not injured. My life was a topic of a disaster. What I could see were tears, always tears.

The person I would never want to hurt, the only person I would fight for with my last blood to defend, was my mother. She disowned me and told me to go find the road where I came from. She was manipulated by religion. I could not help it, and this increased my hatred for myself. I tried to change and behave like I was straight just to get my mother's support, but I just couldn't be a different person from who I am. It killed every vibe in me to hear my mother call me a long-forgotten child and to see how she was able to accept that I did not stay inside her for nine months. Neither did she remember that I sucked her breasts for more than twelve months because of *who I am*, not *who I chose to be*.

It was easy to change from what you learn, not what you were given from birth. My life was a lesson to be learned. It was a chapter of a sociology textbook to teach and a traumatic experience I do not wish for anyone.

All these while in Nigeria, I had lived a blind life—a life of depression, confusion, intimidation, harassment, threats, blackmails, and trauma. With all that, I still pretended to smile, and I thought hopefully, *It will get better for me to live locked inside me.* My tears had been my companion since my sixteenth birthday. Most of the questions I asked myself were, Why is everyone taking me as a strange being? Why am I existing to face pains? Am I truly a curse? I was questioning my existence. This was how I felt. It has been too much for me to take, but I still couldn't find the easy ways to explain to them that I was not the person they see me to be and that I am Jessie Dray, a boy born naturally as everyone else—a gay.

I was born and identified as a man, but I have lived my whole life as a woman inside—a woman full of life and feelings trapped inside. I have never thought or learned from a friend to be a transgender, which I am able to identify as today because I am free in America. I grew up to see myself acting, feeling, and demonstrating as a woman. I have never had the sexual feeling for a woman. There was something the world would not understand—especially my country, Nigeria—and that was feelings. Your feelings are what you are. If you don't have feelings over something, you will never have it. You may have tried as I did, but you will find yourself being a shadow to something, putting yourself to the bondage of trials. It came to a point that I could not control my feelings. I let it loose after forcing myself to be a woman lover for my parents to accept me. Well, it was a movie without an end. I was caught with my boyfriend, kissing, and that was what made me become an exile from Nigeria and from my parents.

Because of that scene, I regretted seeing myself in a mirror because it seemed I saw a strange being in me. I began to live from one's home to another, traveling from one community to another, just to secure a living and to save my life. But it was not as easy as I thought. This gave me depression for years, and I lost my mind.

Today I am happy; I am beginning to see myself as crime-free and offense-free, as a person of a different gender expression. Coming to the United States of America for safety reasons had brought me to see the truth about me.

"I am not a curse, and I have never been a mistake to the world."

The United States had given me reasons why I have the right to speak and move freely, and I was given the opportunity to regain all my losses—my education, my career—and to achieve my dreams. I pray and I hope my country and parents would learn from the miseries and pain they caused their children to go through. God bless, America.

HOW I BECAME AN ACTIVIST

In 2013, I graduated from Enugu State University, Department of Food Science and Technology, Faculty of Agriculture. I believed it was the end of my suffering, humiliation, and shame. Then came the call to serve. Every graduate from a Nigerian university, home or abroad, participates in a one-year compulsory youth service corps program by the federal government. It included three weeks of campaigning and nine months of practice, and the purpose of this program was to unite a divided country of 250 major ethnic groups by posting people to cities very far from their city of origin to learn the local cultures and integrate with their ways of life. It seemed smart, but a country filled with corrupt leaders would only use this opportunity to fill their pockets. Lagos and Abuja were prized; to be sent to these cities, your parents have to be highly placed or you have to have money to bribe a few corps members to get the rare opportunity by chance. I was posted to Niger State, the closest to FCT, and to crown it all up, parts of Abuja were interwoven into Niger State. This was what brought me to Northern Nigeria, where you find a majority of Muslims. Niger State practiced Sharia law, and it was noticeably the largest state in the country by landmass. After three weeks of campaigning, we were posted. I was posted to the interior of the state, the border town between Niger State and Kebbi State, a town named Rijua in Magajiya. Staying in this rural community changed how I saw things. Here were very happy people with poor electricity, a bad water supply, and no health-care facility. Niger State had a vast landmass and was one of the highest producers of root crops, such as yam. Skilled rural farmers used the seasons to plant yams and beans. The name Nigeria came from the word *niger* and the Niger River flows across Niger State. The Zuma Rock and the Gurara Waterfalls were found in this state, for Niger State was blessed by nature and was a center for tourism. It was the powerhouse of Nigeria's electricity with the Kainji Dam, which was designed to have a generating capacity of 960 MW. The dam generates electricity for all the large cities in Nigeria. Some of the electricity is sold to the neighboring countries of Niger. However, Northern Nigeria is known for few educational scholars, and it cannot match the power and brainpower of the south.

I took it upon myself to mobilize corps members to advocate and educate the village women. This was where my activism was born as I organized health education in the public market, using the little Hausa language I had learned to support my current employer at the School of Health Technology in Tungan Magajiya, Rijau. All stacked up in a van, we corps members formed musical instruments with sticks and steel containers and had cardboard sheets we had written with "HIV nor they kill person." HIV does not kill. There is a lot of stigma with doing this kind of work in a country where people living with HIV are kept in a different place and family and friends refuse to share anything with them. I personally related with this stigma, and the lack of acceptance of the LGBT community received this spark—my search for a nonprofit that advocated for the human rights and health access for LGBT folks.

CHAPTER SEVEN

Life after Detention

I was granted a new birth after spending 2,422,000 min. in the womb of immigration detention, so I was not surprised to know that April 18 was World Earth Day. The long wait for Mother Nature to deliver a survivor was just as perfect as the procedure. John Muir wrote, "Nature's peace will flow into you as sunshine flows into trees." It was difficult to spend such a large amount of time in a particular place, but the lessons I learned could not be taught in a classroom. I learned patience was a virtue. I had a wonderful time meeting a new friend, Lillian, who made me understand how valuable it was to be at peace with ourselves and who taught me the practice of studying and listening to myself breathe. The inflow and outflow of air through my lungs had taught me to be calm when everything did not seem to fit together. Many leaders who had changed the world from Africa had spent time in prisons, making an impact in the outside world: Nelson Mandela of South Africa, who fought so hard for his country freedom; Anwar Sadat of Egypt, who led the peace talk with Israel; and Olusegun Obasanjo, who was Nigeria's first democratic president. Olusegun Obasanjo had a bad record for corruption, but he helped Nigeria in achieving democratic governance from military regimes.

I was given a bed at the shelter in Newark, New Jersey, and I could finally sleep in a bed and not on the iron flat bunk I had used to enjoy for the last 173 days. The bunk bed was going to be shared with a stranger, so I dropped off my bag and decided to take a stroll to see some of the beauty of America before I went to sleep. I had not been able to do sightseeing since I was brought to the shelter by bus, the same way I was taken from the airport to the detention center. When I got to the hallway, there were some occupants of the shelter watching a basketball game on television. I just stood and kept quiet, looking at them and trying to feel the excitement they had watching basketball. Then I tried to ask for directions from the social worker on my floor. She had a desk like a receptionist, and I asked her how I could get something to eat. There was a guy standing close to her desk, leaning some part of his body on the desk as a means of support, and he quickly turned and asked me, "Are you from Nigeria?"

"Yes," I replied.

He smiled and said, "Oh, my boy, I am from Cameroon." He had also been brought to the shelter by First Friends.

We exchanged greetings and spoke in pidgin English. He asked what I wanted from the lady and offered to help me navigate that night. He asked me to request a change of room so we could be together, so we made an application to the supervisor for a change of room. But the supervisor had closed his office that night, so the social worker asked me to spend the night in the Cameroonian room and said we could sort things out the next morning. Of course, I was happy to have met someone from the same continent. We started a conversation as he walked me outside to look for a light meal for me to able to sleep well that night. The detention center released detainees at night for reasons best known to them, but I felt it was a strategy for detainees not to be able to recognize the place they had been in for a long time.

My new friend's name was Ari, and he was detained at the Essex County detention center, a different detention center from the one where I was placed. Ari stayed longer than me in his detention center. His asylum case was denied. His immigration attorney made an appeal to the federal court, which granted him approval to revisit his case, and the judge finally granted him asylum after more than a year in the detention center. That was approximately four hundred days he spent in one particular place without seeing the outside world. Ari was granted asylum two weeks before me, so he was more familiar with the outside world and was there to help me feel more comfortable that night. We walked around shops close to the shelter but could not find something very cheap for me to eat, something within the range of three dollars that was at least warm, so Ari told me that he had noodles in the room. If we went back, we could prepare it for me to eat. At the same time, we could return to the shelter before it closed and before we both find ourselves sleeping outside.

Ari used the microwave to heat the noodles, and we had a noodle soup dinner together smiling, grateful for the singular fact that we were no longer in the detention center. I thanked him for his support, and he was glad to have been able to support a brother.

I stayed awake, thinking of where I would go from this place and how I would resettle now that I was out. I opened my bag and took out some of the letters I had received while I was detained, planning to write to these people the next morning that I had been released, especially my friend Lillian, who was waiting to hear of the outcome of my case. Those letters I read made me smile as I shed some tears of joy and felt hopeful that the ability I had to hold on, which had sustained me through detention, would also prove worthy if I could be more resilient now. Sleep was easy to come when I lay on the big foam bed, an experience I had missed and longed for outside the wall of a detention center.

I was woken up by Ari earlier than I expected because we had to go for breakfast in the church pantry. If we didn't go before 8:30 a.m., there would be nothing left for us. He asked me for the paper that was given to me by the lady who had picked me up from the detention center. In the paper, it was written that meals were served by the church pantry from 6:30 a.m. to 8:30 a.m. We were running late. Ari said, "Look for warm clothes to wear, wash your face, and let's go." Ari had a Nigerian friend in Essex County that was transferred to my detention center, and as we were walking to the food pantry, I told him I had met the guy before leaving the detention center. He was so happy to hear of him because he thought he had been deported. When an immigration officer wants to deport some individuals, they arrive as early as 2:00 a.m. and pick up the folks so other detainees will not share emotions as they leave. I told him of the struggle the Nigerian shared with me. He had been detained for over eighteen months. His family had asked him to return because his mother died. Alli had this trauma to deal with while he was still in detention.

We got to the food pantry and lined up. We had gotten there on time, and I was complaining of the length of time we had to wait before it was our turn. Ari told me that some of the homeless people even stayed close to the food pantry as early as 5:40 a.m. I was amazed by the amount of people who were homeless in America. I had had the perception that everything worked fine on the other side. I was also happy that the church provided such a kind opportunity to feed the homeless as this was the example laid down in the Bible and not the bigotry thought by Nigerian religious leaders. The breakfast was luxurious for homeless people like myself at the time. Thanks to the people who contributed for the meals that helped sustain hundreds of homeless people, we had omelets, bagels, croissants, and a choice of beverage—tea and coffee.

We returned to the room with our bellies filled and with ourselves ready to take up the task for the day. Ari was going to use the public library in Newark, New Jersey, and he asked me to join him. I did not want to go to a library to read or pick up a book when my mind was not settled, but I realized he had told me the night before that there would be internet access in the library when I asked him how I could check my Facebook page and emails.

The library in Newark was massive, with historic monuments of the war and of people from Newark that died as a result of the war. I felt the heroics in the building because a warrior recognizes other warriors when they see one. We got an hour each of browsing time to do whatever we wanted to do on the internet. This was gold. The internet cost a lot in my country now, and here I was, being given free access for an hour. I sat there, trying to remember my password and log-in details. I spent almost an hour trying to access my Facebook and ended up not being able to connect with anybody. I became worried that the internet at the shelter was not working, and I could not use the internet again until Friday because I only had access to one hour a day.

Ari came and consoled me. "Let's go and see the outside world. It is a big world here in America, with so many things for you to see."

We hit the road of Newark to try to get me a SIM card with all the money I had, and we moved from one shop to another, asking different retail mobile companies of their cheapest plan. Ari was tired of my bargaining and asked me to choose from one of the previous four stores we had visited.

The day was getting dark, and we had not used the gym for that day, and it was free, so Ari encouraged me to put on shorts so we could use the gym. Then we hit the gym right away. I recalled the experience of using the gym at the detention center, spending an hour in the gym and releasing your negative energies to the metal weight stacks.

I could not feel any better now than how I felt from those days. I knew I was now free, and I had to hustle my way through and become part of the system.

The Friday I was prepared to go to the library to contact my Facebook friends, one significant thing happened in my life on that twenty-second day of April 2017. It was a story I would live to tell in years to come. I hurried to the library with Ari that morning, but little did I know that I wouldn't be able to use the internet. I got a call from Sally, the lady from First Friends, that it was time to go and apply for my social security card. I had to make a choice, and the priority now was not to contact people but to hustle and get my documents to allow me to work and start a new life. Sally took Ari and me for our SSN application. Ari, who had arrived two weeks before me, had never bothered about the SSN as he was comfortable sharing food with the homeless, paying no rent in the shelter, and using the public library internet. I had just gotten released two days before and was eager to get my application rolling. Sally asked me of my work in Nigeria, and I told her of my advocacy work. Then she informed me of First Friends' upcoming dinner and luncheon and how she wanted me to speak on behalf of the postreleased detainees. I gladly accepted, not knowing the number of people that would attend this event. We completed the application at the Social Security office with pretty much ease, considering that I had heard that the lines were usually long on Fridays. Then Sally took Ari and me to the office and gave us some money to use for our transportation.

I now had a cell phone and mobile carrier, and I started messaging my friends back home that I had been granted a stay in America. I posted a picture of me and Ari on my social media account. Many of my friends who had refused writing me letters in the detention center started messaging me. I felt emotional at how people can turn their backs on you when you really need them and then change when things are better for you. I got some cash from Sally and thought, *Now it is time to give myself a good treat and search for a Nigerian restaurant close by and have a taste of home away from home.* The search was shocking as there was a Nigerian restaurant less than five miles from the point I was standing at Newark Penn Station, a fairly walkable distance, so I decided to walk to the restaurant that evening to celebrate my first major step in America and reduce the cost of spending one dollar and sixty cents from the money for bus fare.

I felt excited at the idea of having homemade food after spending such a long time having low-quality meals continuously for more than five months, and when finally I got to the place, a sign was attached to the front roof, announcing Lagos Restaurant. "Hmm, yum yum," my stomach said.

Lagos is the most populated city in Africa and is the hub of African entertainment. I got prepared for a nice meal as I presumed the restaurant was a typical Nigerian restaurant, meaning it has no waiters, with the owner of the restaurant as the waiter, accountant, and person who spearheaded the cooking procedure by giving commands to the chefs from her seat. I took a seat and expected a waiter to attend to me, but she sat in her chair and yelled to her cooks for one of them to come and attend to the customer, who was me. The guy came and handed me the menu. On the menu was a list of my choice—jollof rice, fried plantain, and chicken. I ordered the food, and I could hear my stomach singing in preparation. It all felt like home to some extent because I could hear people speaking local Nigerian dialects and there were pictures of our current leaders and some African images on the walls.

I had the food I had ordered, and it did not taste as great as my mother's holiday jollof rice. But for me, it was better than the frozen food I had been eating since I arrived, and the fish tasted better than the fish cake I had had in Elizabeth. Neither did it taste so sweet like the sugar-coated foods eaten in American fast-food places. My stomach was filled with the large portions, and as I proceeded to pay my bill, I was on the phone with a friend who was asking me how I felt. My response was "It is better to be a free gay man in America." When she heard this statement, you should have been there with me and seen the way the lady looked at me, just like a typical religious Yoruba Nigerian lady. I believe if it was not America and that I had no freedom of speech, she would have spat on my face.

Life had changed, and I was not taking my freedom for granted. So many Africans, Asians, and South Americans immigrate to the United States and continue to be trapped in the shell of family and friends in their home country. I defined these people as debtors to freedom.

VISIT TO THE DETENTION CENTER

I got connected to Ronke, a Nigerian lady in Newark, a friend to a Nigerian detained at the same detention center I was detained in, and she asked me to join her to visit her friend. When I informed Ari of this opportunity, he agreed to join her because his friend, the Nigerian I told him of, was still detained at Elizabeth. I did not want to return to the detention center so soon as I had just gotten released a few days before and was still trying to forget the images of Elizabeth. But I also had friends who had given me their alien number to visit them. Ronke, who had a car, volunteered to give us a ride if we joined her. She wanted me to join because I had experience and relationships with some officers there, and she wanted me to also provide advice and guidance to her friend. When we got to Elizabeth, I was very emotional, standing in front of the detention center. I wanted to visit my friend Mohamed from Liberia, a survivor of the Ebola crisis and a target of his government for protesting the right to treatment for his affected community members. When I saw the windowless gray cinder-block warehouse where I had been living in for the previous five months and fourteen days, I could not hold back the tears that rolled from my eyes. I was holding myself from expressing the joy of being on the outside and not on the other side of that wall. We got through the security checks after dropping our phones and other metal materials, and we were almost treated like detainees, all in an effort to discourage visitors to return.

When my friend Mohamed walked into the visitation room and saw me, he could not say a word; he stood, motionless, seeing me wearing different clothes from the white T-shirt and blue jumpsuit. I walked up to him and gave him a hug and could feel the tears dropping on my shirt, for he could not hold back the pain. He had been detained nine months before me, and I had stayed six months with him, so he had stayed fifteen months in that particular warehouse. I was not strong enough to control my emotions as I had just left five days before. I burst into tears, remembering how it was for me when my friends came to visit me after release. I spoke with Mohamed about life in detention and how he was keeping his mind together because when I was with him, Mohamed was always a man of faith and was persistent in his prayers to Allah for strength. He spoke to me with a smile, "Allah has been there for me, my man."

I wondered again why people who have struggled and fought were rewarded with such traumatic experiences, traumatizing them again. If I had the power to make a difference, I would have made that change in policy that moment, for I know how people were suffering and how they became mentally unstable living daily in isolation.

FLASHBACK ON MY PARENTS

My parents treated me badly, but I began to realize they had a past, and it greatly shaped how they behaved. My dad's actions resulted from his tradition as an Urhobo man, and part of their beliefs was that men should not get married to just one woman. He was pressured by his mother after my mom's cesarean section. In the process of delivering the child that was supposed to be my younger brother, the baby had died. My dad wanted more children after my mom had given birth to four beautiful kids—two boys and two girls—because my dad's mother did not consider the cost of taking care of these children but thought just like in the days of her time when men's wives gave birth to as many children as they could and believed that one of them would be successful. My dad saw only the tip of his nose and did not look beyond. He got a lady pregnant out of wedlock, and she gave birth to two children for my dad—one boy and a girl. Then my dad became less caring toward my mom's children, and we did not know he had a child out of wedlock. Just after the war subsided, he brought the lady to our home and told the entire family he would be officially paying for her bride-price (wedding). This news was shocking, and I believe it affected the way my elder brother and sisters responded, but I was living with my aunt then.

My mom became too protective of me, fearful of losing me, her youngest child, and this led to her rebuking me when she heard news about my sexuality. My mother held me in high esteem. I was her jewel, her baby, and she would do nothing to harm me. She was so protective of me. When my dad came up with the idea to divorce my mom, I was in college. My dad lied that he was breaking up with my mom because she was supporting me and my behavior and that all her kids were wayward.

He kicked my mom out of the house and brought in his new wife and children, and this really affected my mother. She became traumatized, but she still let me remain a part of her life. She told me one evening when I was with her that she saw me as her child and husband. I was happy when she made that statement, but now I see she had been traumatized by the experience and used me to empathize with her for her trauma. My mother was very industrious; she was a successful businesswoman by definition, but my dad was also threatened by her industrious nature and lied to his family that he was divorcing her because he suspected she was sleeping with her customers. She was greatly affected by the divorce, and she had to stop her business and then stay at home doing nothing. Now I began to feel the love of my mother like I had never felt it before, for I was still harboring feelings of survival and resentment from how I had been treated. I would not have understood this past and the story of my parents if I had not taken time to write about my childhood.

STATUE OF LIBERTY

I told my immigration attorney and Batman I didn't want to do activism work anymore because of what I had suffered in Nigeria. I could not imagine how people whom I helped turned their back on me and treated me like my life was not worth living. Ari and I visited New York City, and we heard of the company that helped people with job placements in Staten Island. I also wanted to pick up my judge's order granting me asylum, so it was a win-win for both of us to visit the city.

When my lawyer saw me, he was filled with smiles. He said to me, "Young man, you look handsome and no more in your jumpsuit."

I picked up the letter, amazed by the buildings in the city, the subway system, and the Staten Island Ferry. The ferry passed the Statue of Liberty. I saw a woman holding a torch over her head on her right hand; it resonated with the letter my immigration attorneys wrote to me in detention.

The experience of going by the Statue of Liberty made me rethink my decision. The lady was standing in isolation in the middle of the water, but she still shined strength to the entire city. I might be alone here in the United States, but I could shine light to the issue that most people were ignorant about. As for the people who had made me feel hurt by not writing me letters, I had a different look at the situation and realized that this was due to institutionalized phobia. They were afraid of the system and the consequences of their actions in a very homophobic place.

FIRST FRIENDS' BENEFIT DINNER

On the night I was to present my first speech after the experience, gathered in the hall were about 250 people ready to celebrate postreleased detainees and the work we do in supporting detainees and volunteers who visit detention centers. The state of New Jersey had sixteen counties participating in the detention program. I felt tense speaking about the experience in detention, but with the support of friends who were detained and were eager to let their voices be heard, I had been chosen as a representative. I felt honored when I was called to the stage to speak. I was tense and did not know how to represent the experiences of everyone, but I gave a personal account of my experience, which related also to the experiences of many who had passed through the system.

The lady who was a special guest entertainer also played stories of asylee children and adults from different parts of the world, and I began to heal from my past, knowing that I was not the only one who had been treated that way, that a whole generation was suffering because of the colonial era and laws their parents and family grew up in. I got a glimpse of the world out there for immigrants. The narrative stated how difficult it was to integrate into a new society, but I now felt ready to fight for my spot.

REUNION WITH MY FRIEND

I got a call from my friend Christina on Facebook. She came to Nigeria to participate in the gay men health study in Abuja. I had met her then and told her of my experience as a Nigerian gay man and how difficult it had been for me. She also published some of her studies about the mental health and stigma gay Nigerian men faced. I told her that I was currently living at the shelter, and she offered me to come and stay with her in New York City. She offered me support to find my feet in a new country and told me of her struggles of being a person of color who studied in a white-dominated university. She gave me an orientation and asked me to start by reading about the culture of blacks to help me understand it was not easy for immigrants.

When I got to New York City the first day, excited by my new life, she stood by me, and I could not forget the support she and other friends provided in making life in the United States worth living. It was not easy to stay with a guy, but she provided me a space without grudges and never took a penny from me. I stayed with her for a reasonable period of time until I could stand on my own feet.

MY FIRST JOB IN NEW YORK CITY

I started looking for a job when I got my working document, but I was growing impatient of looking for a blue-collar job. Many immigrants like myself start in the city with factory and security jobs, so I went to a job placement agent and paid some money for them to look for a job for me. When I got the response from the job placement industry, I had been invited to do a job at a factory in Long Island City at a grocery factory to work as a helper and arrange fruits into cartons. I was happy to take the job because I had been encouraged not to bother looking for better jobs since everyone must have a start. I ended up not taking the job because I have a master's in nutrition and I would not accept the narrative that I was not good enough for a more professional American job.

Staying at home was not helping me, so I joined a group that went on a street campaign as a canvasser to ask for people to support funds for equality. I did it one day, and I was assigned to Bowling Green Park. All day, I was seeing the Statue of Liberty and remembering the resilience that the torch she held meant for me to shine. I called in the next day that I was not going to continue street canvassing.

I continued my job search with the refugee resettlement agency who sent me to interviews as a cleaner in a hotel or assistant at a warehouse where female clothes were packaged, but I did not hear from those interviews I did because my résumé indicated my education was higher than what they wanted.

I was in the city one day in June when the sun came out, and I visited Times Square and was just sitting in the stands when I received a call from the refugee resettlement agency that a kitchen was looking for a manager and that I was fit for the position. I ran to the interview, which would take place the same day by noon, and although I was not dressed for an interview or prepared mentally for the interview, my résumé showed my educational experiences as a food scientist and nutritionist. The CEO spoke with me about the company, and their mission really matched with my vision. It was an all-refugee agency that provided authentic ethnic foods prepared by refugees. I accepted to start by Monday, and over the weekend, I told my roommate of this opportunity. We were very happy. The kitchen was in Long Island City and was very close to the place where I lived—just two train stops.

On Monday, I began work, and the beautiful part of my experience was meeting the chefs who were from different parts of the world, fleeing persecution from Syria, Nepal, Iran, Eritrea, etc. This became my new family. I believed I was brought here for a reason, and I believed this was part of my story of integration in America.

LETTER FROM THE AUTHOR

Life had been different since I came out of detention. I never imagined my life would ascertain such freedom in less than a year from my release date. I had been able to integrate into the society easier than I predicted. I heard it takes some refugee an average of seventeen years to resettle. I am not where I want to be in life now, but I am grateful for the steps I have taken so far.

I was elected as a board member of First Friends of New Jersey and New York, and I continued to advocate for the marginalized and oppressed immigrants detained. I was accepted as a fellow of Columbia University's department of social justice as a Beyond the Bars Fellowship major feet to study prison reforms and criminal justice systems. I attended the United Nations' youth assembly, presented a speech at the United Nations, and supported the community the best way I could. Eat Offbeat completed its cookbook featuring refugees from different parts of the world. I joined Hyacinth AIDS Foundation and continued my advocacy for access to care for the LGBT community.

I was independent in my actions, and I continued to organize on the streets of New York and New Jersey and protested against unjust systems. The most powerful political and self-expressing tool is writing. That's why I documented my account to encourage young people and older people as well to continue to stand up for what is right.

I feel very confident of myself. With the love and support from my friends, allies, colleagues who are too many to mention, and people from different races, religious beliefs, sexual orientation, and gender identities, life could not be more enjoyable with these people in my life. I continue to fight as it is not over yet. Millions of people around the world are still being persecuted, and we need to support them as much as we can and see an end to inequality.

Printed in the United States
By Bookmasters